# THE SHERIFF'S OMEGA

## C.W. GRAY

CONTENTS

# CHAPTER 1

"I've never seen anything like this, Sheriff," Parker, one of Mack's deputies, said, face drawn with worry.

"Who would do this kind of thing?" Tanner, another deputy, asked, hands braced on his hips as he took in the sight before them.

Mrs. Turnbell had called it in early this morning, right when Mack was sitting down with his morning coffee. That's when he knew today was going to be a long day. Small towns were supposed to be easy to handle, or so he'd been told. Mack had grown up in Hobson Hills, though. He should have known better.

"I know who did this." Mack took a drink of his coffee. "We all know who did this."

"Ernie," the two deputies said together.

"Yep." Mack shook his head at the sight in front of him. Someone, probably Ernie Wilson, had put knitted bonnets and scarves on the Turnbells' cattle. One brown-and-white heifer even wore bright-pink leg warmers.

Tanner sighed. "Last night at the pub, Mr. Turnbell told

Ernie that Bigfoot doesn't exist. I've never seen Ernie so mad. Honestly, I don't think Mr. Turnbell cares about Bigfoot being real or not. He just likes to see Ernie's face turn red."

"Should we dust for fingerprints?" Parker asked, dark eyes twinkling with laughter. "Bag the knitted goods?"

Mack grunted and took another long drink of coffee. "You two get in there and take those things off the cattle. I'll talk to Mrs. Turnbell."

*She makes a good cup of coffee too*, Mack thought, looking mournfully into his empty cup. If the Wilsons were already stirring, then today really would be a long day. He needed more caffeine.

"I'm too old for this shit," he muttered, striding up the Turnbells' steps.

Mrs. Turnbell stood in the doorway, a fresh cup of coffee in her hands. "Here you go, Sheriff."

Mack gratefully took the cup and leaned back against the porch rails. "Sorry about this, Angie. My boys will take care of the cattle."

She rolled her eyes with a huff. "I told Phil that he shouldn't have riled up Ernie like that. If he wasn't such an old man, I'd have made him take care of the cattle. He'd likely throw out his back though."

"Hey now, I'm not that old." Phil sat on the porch swing with a book in his lap. "She just likes to watch those boys move."

Mack laughed and looked over his shoulder. Tanner and Parker were chasing the heifer with the leg warmers at the moment. She didn't seem to want to part with her new outfit.

"They do move well," Angie said with a grin. "I remember when you used to be that energetic, Mack, chasing after Darren like a new puppy. I had the hardest time keeping the two of you apart in class. My two favorite students."

He smiled, enjoying the memories. Darren had been gone for years now, but Mack had never stopped loving him. He never would.

"How are Lacey and Renee?" Angie asked, giving him a fond smile.

"Bossy and nosy," Mack said with a huff. "All they talk about is how I need to retire and 'enjoy my twilight years.'"

Phil laughed loud enough to startle the cattle, unfortunately for Tanner, who had just managed to remove one leg warmer from the heifer.

"You aren't even sixty yet," Angie said, shaking her head. "She must think us ancient, Phil."

"You *just* said I was an old man." Phil pouted. "If Mack is in his twilight years, then we're ready for the grave."

Angie leaned next to Mack and nudged his side. "You know what you really need?"

"To move to a quiet town where nobody knows me?" he asked hopefully.

"Nope." Angie patted his arm. "You need to start dating again. Maybe if your life was more than work, your girls wouldn't think you were a doddering old man."

"I date," Mack protested with a sniff.

"The occasional dinner out with a friend isn't dating," Angie said, sighing.

Mack winced. He knew that. After Darren passed away, Mack hadn't wanted to get close to anyone else. Losing his husband had hurt. Plus, he knew there wasn't much of a chance that he would ever find a love like he'd had with Darren. Dating didn't seem worth it.

Phil chuckled and pointed toward the pasture. Tanner was covered in mud and manure, but he had all the leg warmers off the heifer. He raised them in the air with a shout of victory. Parker saluted him before chasing after a calf that didn't want to part with its scarf.

Mack drank the last of his coffee and set his cup down. "I better go help, or we'll be here all day."

Angie leaned up to kiss his cheek. "Think about what I said, Mack. You should have more to look forward to in life than chasing cattle around the pasture."

Mack grinned as he ducked through the fence. Maybe he would get out more, and maybe he wouldn't. He was content with his life. At the very least, it was never boring living in Hobson Hills.

By LUNCHTIME, Mack was ready for a break. All the cattle had been put to rights, and he was on the way to take the knitted items back to Ernie.

He pulled into the gravel drive leading to Ernie's home and eyed the man's front porch. A dog gate blocked off the steps, but Mack could see Ernie lounging in a chair with his youngest son, Maury. Clover and Anthony, Ernie's twins, crawled around the porch, chasing their big dog, Pudge.

Mack parked his car and grabbed the bag of knitted items before making his way to the porch.

"Well, would you look at that, kids," Ernie said, a mischievous smile covering his face, "our favorite sheriff brought some gifts."

Anthony crawled to the gate and grinned at Mack, holding his arms up.

Mack grunted and set the bag down so he could pick up the little boy. "You're lucky these kids are distractingly cute, Ernie Wilson."

"Ernie Wilson-Hart," Ernie corrected primly. "I assume that bag has some knitted scarves and hats ready for donation?"

"After a good wash." Mack bounced Anthony, grinning as the little boy laughed. "Sometimes, I miss babies."

Ernie gave him a sly look. "Want me to set you up with a few single omegas? I'd love to see Lacey's face when you tell her that she's going to have a new sibling."

Mack snorted. "Why do the two of you enjoy picking at each other so much? You're both sweet people, but I swear you bring out the worst in each other."

Ernie shrugged. "I can't help it. Everyone needs a nemesis. Mine is a six-foot-tall blonde accountant."

Ernie and Mack's daughter had gone to school together. Ever since they met in grade school, the two had professed their hatred of one another. At first, Mack and Darren had thought their daughter had a crush on Ernie and didn't know how to deal with it. When they had sat down to talk with her, Lacey had quickly explained that boys were gross and that she liked Renee Donahue.

After years of admittedly funny pranks, the two had finally settled into adulthood. Well, mostly. Occasionally, they crossed one another in town and pointedly ignored each other, but at least the active shenanigans were over.

Mack sighed. Now, he just had to worry about Ernie's pranks on cattle, and Lacey's obsession with her upcoming wedding to Renee. It was all she ever talked about, other than those lovely moments when she decided to convince him to retire.

"Make my life easier, Ernie." Mack reluctantly set Anthony down. "Leave the Turnbells' cattle alone."

Ernie's eyes narrowed. "Did Phil Turnbell learn his lesson?"

Mack nodded, one hundred percent lying. "He deeply regrets ever doubting the existence of Bigfoot."

"Good." Ernie stood. "Come in, and I'll make you some lunch. You can play with the babies."

Mack looked at Anthony's cute chubby face. "Deal."

Ernie opened the door. "Reuben made coconut curry last night. Is that good with you?"

"Sounds delicious." Mack herded the twins and Pudge inside. Ernie's husband was an excellent cook, and Mack enjoyed anything the man made.

A few moments later, he sat on the floor in the living room and watched the twins play while he held a sleepy Pudge in his arms. The large dog still thought he was a baby.

Maury watched the twins from his swing, likely planning how to get in as much trouble as possible as soon as he could crawl. The twins were just under one year old and already full of energy. Mack remembered well how active Lacey was at that age. Soon enough, they would be walking, and then Ernie wouldn't have the time to play pranks on anyone. He hoped.

Pudge licked Mack's face before settling his head on his shoulder.

"Yuck." Mack wiped his face with his sleeve. "I was supposed to have babies to play with, not you, Pudge."

Clover crawled to him and patted his leg before chasing after one of Ernie's cats. Anthony giggled and followed behind her.

Ernie's house was small and cozy, with well-loved furniture and way too many knitted items. Dog toys lay beside kids' toys on the central rug, and *Scooby Doo* played on the television. A Roomba went by with a cat riding atop it. This was a place that was comfortable with the life it nourished.

*This is what I miss*, he thought suddenly, a deep ache welling inside him. He missed having a house full of life. When Lacey was grown and moved out, he should have still had Darren beside him, loving him.

"Pudge, I'm starting to feel as old as my daughter and her fiancée think I am," he whispered, patting the dog's back.

His phone rang, and Pudge glared at him, affronted, as if to say *"Turn that damn thing off. I have sleep to get to."*

"Sorry," Mack said with a wince before answering his phone. "Sheriff McKenzie speaking."

"Hi, Sheriff," a man said. "This is Cain Benson. I think you know my parents and my brothers, Carter and Caden."

"Yes, I do," Mack said, smiling. Cain was the youngest of his brothers and the only one who still worked in the family law firm in Georgia.

"I have a favor to ask," Cain said, voice grim. "It's important."

"What can I do for you?" Mack asked, already knowing he'd do everything he could to help the man. The Bensons were good people, and Mack genuinely liked them.

"I need a safe place for a client and his family to stay for a few months." Cain's anger carried through his voice. "Someone is trying to kill him."

# CHAPTER 2

"*D*ad, you could have died." Tris paced back and forth in front of the large picture window in the sitting room. "We could have lost you."

Roe swallowed hard, body aching from the injuries he'd sustained in the accident. "I'm aware, sweetheart."

"We're going to Hobson Hills to stay with Mr. Benson's friend," Daphne said, curling closer against his side while being careful of the bruising on his chest and abdomen. "Even if we have to stay there forever, we will, Daddy. We can't lose you."

Roe hugged her, hating the fear in her voice. It had been years since she called him *Daddy*.

"That *man* got everything he wanted in the divorce," Tris said, unwilling to say his alpha father's name aloud. "What else do he and his new arm candy want?"

"They should be totally happiful," Daphne muttered against Roe's shoulder.

Instead, Roe's ex-husband, James, and his new husband, Gabriel, were doing their best to make Roe's life a living hell. It had started small with rumors being spread among Roe's wealthy friends. All complete garbage lies, but Roe had learned a long time ago that some friends were fickle at best. In their eyes, it was more entertaining to support the lovely Gabriel. Not only was he gorgeous, the other man was also a social butterfly. Everyone loved him.

"Just like Eleanor and Rosamund," Roe muttered.

"What?" Daphne asked, confused.

"I'm Eleanor of Aquitaine, and Gabriel is Rosamund Clifford," Roe explained. "You know, 'The Fair Rosamund.'"

"Is this one of your random historical lessons, Dad?" Tris asked, sighing.

"Maybe." Roe scowled. "Everyone loved Rosamund."

Gabriel had a way about him that drew people in. It didn't matter that James and Gabriel's affair had gone on for five years before Roe finally noticed his husband's cheating and filed for divorce. It didn't seem to matter that James had signed away his rights to the kids in exchange for Roe's family business—the business Roe's grandfather had built from the ground up, where his father and mother had tirelessly worked to make it one of the most elite investment firms in the country.

Roe missed his parents and grandparents tremendously, but he was glad they hadn't been around when the mess with James started. They didn't have to see their company go to a heartless vulture. He knew they would approve of him using it to keep the kids, though. Family was the most important thing to the Dorseys.

"Did Rosamund try to hire someone to kill Eleanor?" Cain asked, leaning forward and bracing his arms on his knees. "We know Gabriel did."

"That was two years ago." Roe winced.

James and Gabriel hadn't been content with Roe losing all his friends. Anonymous threats had followed. A disgusting letter left in his mailbox, a nasty email sent from a fake address. That's when Roe had gone to Cain, a family friend. Cain's law firm included a top-notch criminal lawyer.

They had done everything they could, but at first, there wasn't much to do. They didn't know who was to blame. Then, Gabriel had gotten caught trying to hire someone to kill Roe. Thankfully, the "hired killer" had been an undercover police officer.

Roe had been so relieved that the nastiness was finally over, but being caught in the act hadn't mattered in the end. Gabriel had batted his eyes and swore that it had all been a misunderstanding, and James had said it was just a joke. Gabriel had been released with a warning. A month later, Roe's mechanic had noticed his brake lines had been cut. Luckily, movies had it wrong. He hadn't even gotten out of the driveway before he noticed his brake pedal had gone soft and the indicator light came on. Nothing could be traced to Gabriel or James, but Roe had been careful to keep his car in the garage after that. Then, things had gotten better. They had been careful to stick with nonviolent harassment like the letters and rumors.

Today, however, a truck had run his car off the road and into a deep ravine. Roe had never been so frightened in his life. He still heard Fergie's yelps from the back seat. Fortunately, Fergie's seat harness had kept him from flying through a window.

"Fergie could have died too," Tris said softly, slumping onto the couch beside them.

Roe wrapped an arm around his son's shoulders. "We're all okay, son."

Roe had a broken nose, black eyes, bruised ribs, and a fractured ankle. His whole body ached, but he was alive. Fergie was curled up on his dog bed, sore and tired himself. The vet had cleared him and told them the dog had been extremely lucky.

They would have been a lot worse off if another car hadn't come upon them. The young couple in it had gotten a good look at the truck and even a partial license plate number before it drove off. Waiting for help had been excruciating. He couldn't move, couldn't help Fergie. Cain had beat the ambulance to the accident site, and Roe had never been so happy to see him.

"I already called Sheriff McKenzie," Cain said, his voice tired. "He's happy to help and has plenty of room for everyone." He pointedly looked toward the corner of the room. "Everyone."

"I don't need a bodyguard," Roe groaned, neck twinging as he looked toward the corner. "No offense, Wally."

"None taken." Wally smiled, arms crossed in front of him. "I'm still not leaving."

The professional bodyguard had been waiting at the house when Roe finally got home. Cain moved quickly—so quickly that Roe suspected he'd had Wally contracted before the accident.

The large bald man was an imposing sight at first glance. He was huge and muscled with intricate tattoos covering his bare arms. However, all anyone had to do was look at his warm brown eyes, and they'd know the truth: Wally was a sweetie-pie. Well, a sweetie-pie who could flatten a person if he wanted to.

"We want Wally there," Tris said, leaning his head on Roe's other shoulder. "It makes us feel better."

Roe narrowed his eyes, not completely sure if his son was playing him or being honest.

"We'll pack your bags tonight, even your art supplies," Cain said, jumping to his feet. "You can be on the road by tomorrow."

"What?" Roe scowled. "I haven't—"

"While you're gone," Cain continued, ignoring him, "I'll

have the car looked over for evidence and stay on top of the police investigation. We'll find what we need."

Roe stared at his friend for a moment. If he were to paint Cain, it would be a traditional oil painting with asphaltum shading—somber but warm. A well-worn, comforting presence. He knew Cain was right, but Roe was scared. The thought of leaving his home made him angry. James and Gabriel had kept Roe on edge for years with the constant battering of their threats and scheming. Roe didn't want to run. He'd lived in Loriston for twenty years now, and he didn't want to be chased out of town, damn it.

Cain gave him a knowing look. "This is necessary, Roe. When I arrived, your car was totaled at the bottom of a ravine. Fergie was howling, and I thought you were dead."

"I don't want them to win," Roe whispered, hugging his two eldest children closer to him.

"This isn't a game to win or lose. This was attempted murder." Cain began to pace behind the couch. "I won't let them get away with this. I'll find their connection to the driver of the truck. I just need to know you and the kids are safe in the meantime."

"Benji could have been in the car with you, Dad." Tris sniffled and rubbed his face against Roe's shoulder. "I don't usually pick him up from daycare. You do."

Roe shivered at the thought of his youngest being in the car with him today. Right now, Benji was asleep upstairs, unaware of how close his dad had come to dying. The anger drained from him, leaving behind numb fatigue. He was so tired of being afraid.

"Okay." Roe tightened his hold on Tris and Daphne. "We'll do it."

"Can we bring Mmrr and Fergie?" Daphne asked.

Mmrr lifted her head when she heard her name. The

large fluffy white cat lay on one of the chairs across the room.

"Room for everyone," Cain said, nodding. "Let's start packing. Tris, will you pack up your dad's studio? We'll take two cars, so box up everything."

Tris stood and kissed the top of Roe's head. "On it."

"I'll pack for Benji and the pets." Daphne slowly untangled herself from Roe's hug. "How long will we be gone?"

"Hopefully only a few months." Cain knelt beside Fergie and started gently petting the dog.

"Plan for the rest of the year," Roe said, closing his eyes. "School will start in two months, and I don't want to move you or Benji midsemester."

Daphne danced in place. "That means I get a semester away from St. James Academy. Perfect."

"It's a good school," Roe said, rubbing his forehead. "I still don't understand why you don't like it, but you don't have to go back. We'll try public school in Hobson Hills. At least we'll be closer to Tris when he starts at Harvard."

"We can visit him! It'll be great, Dad. You'll see." She left the room with a determined smile.

"I'll go walk the perimeter." Wally patted Roe's shoulder. "Get as much rest as you can, Mr. Dorsey. It's going to be a long drive."

After he left, Mmrr jumped from her seat and made her way to Roe's lap. Once settled, he began petting her, enjoying her rumbling purrs.

"I'm so tired, Cain." Roe leaned his head against the back of the couch. "Five years of this rancid shit is more than enough. I used to love living here. Everything reminded me of my grandpas. I had friends. I wasn't afraid to leave the house."

Cain sat beside him and pulled him into a hug. "I'm so sorry, Roe."

Roe felt the tears he'd been trying to keep back start to fall. "I don't even know what they want. I'd give them everything except the kids, and I know James doesn't want them. He never did. What else do they want from me?"

"People like that never have enough." Cain sighed. "Your grandpa Roland would be pissed if he was still alive. He thought James was a perfect son-in-law."

Roe snorted. "Grandpa Ben knew he was crap from the moment he met him. I wish I would have listened to him, but James seemed like a dream come true when we met."

He had been the perfect addition to the Dorsey family. Roe had no interest in the family business, but James did. Grandpa Roland and Roe's parents had been thrilled, while Grandpa Ben had delved into James's background and made him sign an ironclad prenuptial agreement.

"I wish they were here now." Cain tightened his arms around Roe. "They would chew him up and spit him out."

Roe patted Cain's chest. "That's your job now. Make them stop, Cain. I don't care what it takes."

"I will," Cain said with icy certainty.

# CHAPTER 3

"*Dad*, why are you doing this?" Lacey asked, hands on her hips. "They're complete strangers who could be con-artists and take advantage of you."

Mack arched a brow. "Baby girl, when has anyone ever been able to take advantage of me? Excluding the Wilsons and Doc Grover, of course."

She nibbled her lip and gave him a worried look. "It's more than letting strangers in your house, though. A man your age doesn't need this kind of responsibility. If someone is really after this Dorsey guy, you could be hurt just by associating with him."

He narrowed his eyes. "Lacey Ann McKenzie, are you saying I should *not* help someone in need?"

Lacey flushed and ducked her head. "It's just that it might be dangerous."

Mack sighed and pulled her into a hug. "Sweetheart, I know you worry, but I can handle myself. I've been doing so for a long time now. This man and his family are in a hard situation. They deserve help, not judgment and fear."

She hugged him back. "You're right. I know you arc."

"Good." Mack leaned back. "Now, help me freshen up the spare rooms. I haven't even looked in them for weeks."

Lacey rolled her eyes. "You really need a smaller place, Dad. They're probably full of dust. How many rooms do you need to have ready?"

"There are five people," he said, making her scowl when he ruffled her hair. "Two adults, two teens, and a toddler."

"*Two* adults? I thought the man and his family were alone."

"Cain is sending a bodyguard with them."

The look of relief on her face shouldn't have annoyed him so much, but Mack was a bit tired of her thinking he was a useless old man.

"That's great," Lacey said, grinning wide. "We should do all three spare rooms and maybe my old room in the attic?"

Mack snorted. "Perfect for a moody teen."

Lacey laughed. "I was so emo."

"My little emo-goth princess." Mack hugged her. "Have I told you how much I love you?"

"Not since this morning." Lacey hugged him back. "I love you too, Dad."

After that, they worked together on the rooms while Lacey rambled about the ideas Barry, her wedding planner, had for the flowers. With anyone else, he'd be miserable, but there were very few things he enjoyed more than listening to his daughter. She had always been open with him, but after Darren died, he and Lacey had grown even closer. She told him everything, whether he liked it or not.

By late afternoon, the house was as clean as it had ever been. Lacey left for home, and Mack took a moment to check in at the station. It had been a long time since he'd taken a day off. He trusted his people and tried not to micromanage them, but he was used to being in control.

His phone beeped, and he read a text from Cain. They were almost to the house.

Mack went outside to wait on the porch. The neighborhood was in the center of town, lined with older, well-kept houses. He had lived there for over thirty years and loved his home. It was an old Victorian with gray-blue shaker siding and white trim. The front yard was small but neat, and he had a larger fenced-in backyard. Perfect for the family he didn't have anymore.

A large black SUV pulled into the driveway, coming to a stop in front of Mack's detached garage. The driver got out and went straight to the back, opening the hatch and grabbing luggage. Mack went to help but paused as another SUV pulled in behind the first, and a man got out.

The man's scent carried on the breeze and screamed "omega." The man was in his late forties, and he had wide shoulders and a nice build, but that wasn't what grabbed Mack's attention. The man's smile was warm and open, and his dark-brown eyes were kind. He also had two black eyes and a bandaged nose.

"Are you Mack?" he asked, coming forward, hand extended. The walking boot made his stride a little awkward, but he still somehow managed to appear graceful.

Mack cleared his throat and gathered himself. "Ian McKenzie. Roland Dorsey?"

The man wrinkled his nose. "Roland was my grandfather. Rally was my dad. I'm just Roe."

"Roe," Mack said, smiling. "Suits you."

"Hey, Sheriff McKenzie." Cain strode toward him, carrying a few suitcases. "Thanks for helping out. No, Roe, don't grab that. You shouldn't be doing any heavy lifting for at least a week, and you really need to stay off your ankle."

Roe groaned and set the suitcase he had grabbed back down. "You're worse than Wally. I feel just fine."

Cain had said Roe had been in an accident recently. He was likely stiff from the ride and in pain.

"Come inside and sit down, Roe," Mack said, hand slipping to the omega's lower back to guide him toward the house.

Roe flushed and coughed. "That sounds good, but I need to get Benji. He fell asleep."

"Go on in." Mack patted his back. "I'll bring your son in."

"Are you sure?" Roe suddenly looked exhausted. "I don't want to impose."

"Come on, Roe." Cain shooed him toward the house. "Mack doesn't mind."

Shaking his head, Mack smiled and went to the SUV. He should probably mind Cain volunteering him, but he liked being useful. Roe needed a break, and Mack was in a position to help. Simple as that.

He stopped at the second SUV, noticing for the first time that two teens were helping the large bald man with the luggage. The boy was an omega in his late teens, and the girl was younger, maybe fourteen or fifteen. With dark-brown hair, olive skin, and kind eyes, both looked a lot like their dad.

The little boy in the back seat, on the other hand, had dark-red hair and freckled golden skin. He lay with his head back, a bit of drool dripping down his chin.

Mack quickly unstrapped Benji and gently picked him up. The little boy barely stirred, and he settled his head on Mack's shoulder.

"They're good people," the bodyguard told him, voice soft. "I'm Wally, by the way."

"Mack," he said, nodding a greeting. "Honestly, it'll be nice to have the company."

"How do you feel about cats?" The teen boy came toward

them, holding a fluffy white cat up for inspection. It stared at him with serene green eyes.

He rubbed his chin and took his time looking the cat over. Hiding his smile, he finally nodded. "This cat will do."

The teenager snorted a laugh. "This is Mmrr, and I'm Tris. That's Daphne there."

Daphne carried a corgi to them. "This is Fergie. The vet said he's okay, but he's in a little pain, so we're not letting him run around like he wants."

Mack gently rubbed the top of the dog's head. "I bet he is. I'll get Doc Grover to come by and look him over. Just in case."

"Oh, that's not necessary," Daphne said, flushing. "He'll be okay."

"It's no trouble." Mack did his best to herd everyone toward the house. The porch was covered with boxes and suitcases. The quiet, empty house wouldn't be so quiet or empty anymore, and Mack loved it.

"Tris, you can set up a litter box in the mud room for Mmrr. It's just down the hall and to the right. Daphne, why don't you and Fergie rest on the sofa? We'll get him a dog bed set up after I take Benji upstairs. A friend brought over a toddler bed, and I got it set up in the corner of your dad's room."

Roe stirred from where he sat in the front room. Despite the battered face, Roe's smile was sweet and warm. "That's perfect. Thank you, Ian."

Mack froze, startled at the sound of his name. Only Darren had ever called him by his first name since his parents passed. To everyone else, he was Mack or Sheriff. The way Roe said it made it seem like more than a name. It was an intimacy.

"Yes, thank you, *Ian*." Cain arched a brow and eyed him. "I'm starting to regret not staying to see how this plays out."

"How what plays out?" Roe asked, yawning as Daphne and Fergie sat beside him.

Cain smirked. "Don't worry about it. Wally, will you keep me updated?"

The large man grinned. "With pleasure."

Mack scowled, confused at the knowing tone in Cain's voice. "Cain, you used to be my favorite Benson."

LATER THAT AFTERNOON, all their belongings were sorted into their respective rooms. Daphne had fallen in love with the attic bedroom, so it was hers, while the others took the guestrooms. The only boxes left were art supplies for Roe.

Mack considered the sunroom, eyeing the empty pots occupying the old plant shelves. Darren had enjoyed gardening and had turned the sunroom into a conservatory. Mack didn't have the time or desire to keep it up, so most of the plants had gone with Lacey when she moved out.

"Would it be too much sun for a studio?" he asked Tris.

"Does it get too warm?" Tris asked, looking around. "It's July, but it's a lot colder here than back home. I think it feels comfortable right now."

Mack nodded. "We can pull the shades if it gets too warm. It gets a little chilly in the winter, but there's a small gas fireplace in that corner. It's enough to keep it comfortable when it's cold out."

"Are you sure you don't mind Dad using it?" Tris asked, giving him a worried look. "We're asking a lot of you already."

Mack snorted. "Does it look like I use this room?"

Tris winced and patted a wilting fern. "Can I take this little guy up to Daphne's room? She loves plants and can probably help it."

"Sure." Mack pulled one of the old plant racks away from the window. "I'll clean up in here and move the art supplies in."

"I can help." Tris took one end of an old wrought iron baker's rack and pulled it toward the door. "Dad couldn't bring his work table and easel, but maybe we can find something in town."

"I'll figure it out. You must be tired from the drive. Don't you want to rest?" Mack had noticed the young man yawning a few minutes ago.

Tris shrugged, the uncertainty on his face making him appear much younger. "I haven't slept in three days," he admitted, voice cracking. "This is insane, right? Maybe I shouldn't leave in August. I can take online classes. He almost *died.*"

Mack couldn't help himself. He pulled the young man into a hug. "We'll keep him safe, Tris."

"I hate my alpha father," Tris said, shuddering. "I hate that I'm named after him. Granted, it's his middle name I took, but he's an asshole, and Gabriel is even worse. Dad doesn't deserve any of this. He's a good person."

"No one deserves this," Mack said, rubbing Tris's back. "One thing I've learned over the years is that all those bad things in life don't discriminate. We can't control that."

Mack looked up when he heard footsteps. Roe stood in the doorway, watching them with a soft look.

"You aren't alone in this," Mack said, not sure if he was talking to Tris or Roe. "I'll do my best to keep you all safe."

# CHAPTER 4

"You really don't have to cook breakfast," Roe said, watching Mack as he flipped a pancake from the pan to a plate. The sheriff had taken the day off again and wore an old, well-worn pair of jeans and a faded gray T-shirt. He was making bacon and pancakes. With Benji's help.

Roe's youngest had only just turned three. He stood on a chair and held the plate still for Mack to fill up. Benji chattered nonstop, fully refreshed from a full night's sleep.

"It's no problem," Mack said, smiling at Roe. "Everyone has to eat, right? Now, tell me more about Pepper and Carrot."

"Pepper on broom," Benji said, wiggling in place. "Carrot kitty flies with."

"Wow," Mack said, grinning. "This is all from a comic?"

Benji nodded. "The best. Daffy read 'em."

Roe struggled not to explode with pride. His little boy loved a good story. He would be reading along with them soon.

"Daphne," she corrected, exasperated. "Daffy is a duck."

Benji blew her a kiss. "Quack, quack, Daffy duck."

Mack's head fell back as he laughed, and Roe stared help-lessly. With his silver and black hair and his strong jaw, the man was gorgeous. Even better, he was kind. Wally made Roe and the others feel safe, but being around Mack made Roe feel at home. If Roe were to paint him, he would be a mixed media oil painting with acrylic. Maybe an under-painting of blues and grays with a darker-hued portrait with texture. Definitely not a traditional canvas. He would shape it himself. Smooth and rolling edges with a custom-made cherry wood frame.

Roe settled his chin onto his fist and enjoyed the laughter filling the kitchen. Last night, he had slept better than he had in years knowing that Wally and Mack would handle any trouble that showed up. Not that he would ever tell Cain that. The alpha already had a big head, and Roe wasn't about to tell him he had been right in sending them here.

"The Book Worm has story time every afternoon for little bits like you, Benji," Mack said, ruffling the boy's hair. "Maybe you can go and bring your comic. I bet the other kids would like *Pepper and Carrot* too."

"Oh, what time?" Daphne asked, brightening. "Is it within walking distance? I can take him, Dad."

Benji clapped. "Please, please."

"It's at one, Monday through Friday." Mack set a plate in front of Roe. "It's only two blocks away, but I can take them if you want me to, Roe."

"You don't have to do that," Roe said, his mouth watering at the sight of all that bacon. "I can take them."

"We could walk," Daphne said, rolling her eyes. "It's just two blocks, Dad."

"It's a new town, sweetheart." Roe groaned as he chewed. Why did pancakes taste so much better when someone else made them?

"I'll walk with them, Dad." Tris yawned and rubbed his eyes. The teen was *not* a morning person, but bacon was enough to get him out of bed.

"Ian, does that sound okay?" Roe asked. "You know your town best."

Mack nodded with a smile. "They'll be fine. I'll let the bookstore know to expect them too."

Roe would have liked to go with them, but he was still hurting quite a bit and could use the rest.

"Deal."

Benji clapped and jumped up and down on the chair, prompting Mack to pick him up and set him down on the floor. "Careful there, Little Bit."

Tris moaned appreciatively as he stuffed his face. "Your pancakes are so much better than Dad's."

Roe snorted and held his hand over his heart. "*Et tu, Brute?*"

Mack grinned. "I like cooking."

"We like eating," Roe said, taking another bite.

Mack sat down across from him, eyes shining with laughter. "We're a good match, then."

The comment warmed Roe more than it should, so he focused on helping Benji into his booster seat. "Remember to use your fork, baby boy."

Benji wrinkled his nose, but he did as he was told.

"Our local vet will be stopping by to take a look at Fergie," Mack said in between bites. "I have a friend bringing you a work table for your art room too. He should be here around noon."

All Roe really wanted was a quiet morning of reading and sketching. His fingers were itching to draw Mack from the back—maybe with the man looking over his shoulder, his blue eyes full of life. If only Roe could get the man to stand still long enough for him to get the lines right.

"I have security people coming by to put in a new system," Wally said, his own plate already clean. "I'll be with Roe the whole time if you need to work, Mack."

The older man grinned. "I want to help Roe get settled, and I have a lot of PTO to use. We're actually hiring a few more people right now, so I have applications to look through. I can do that from here."

Roe rolled his eyes. "I'm a grown man, you know." His frustration softened as he noticed how easily Mack and Wally blended in with his family. "Thank you for arranging for everything, Ian. You too, Wally. I really do appreciate the two of you."

Mack scooped another pancake onto Roe's plate. "Don't thank me yet. Doc Grover will likely try to get you to adopt some pet, and the Wilsons now know you're in town. I'm not sure it'll be a peaceful day for you."

"I'M REALLY NOT sure we need guinea pigs," Roe said, holding two extremely fuzzy guinea pigs against his chest. They wheeked gently, and the black-and-orange one crawled up onto his shoulder.

"Oh, I understand," Doc Grover said, smiling kindly as he stroked Fergie's head. "It's just that they're a bonded pair, and I've had no luck adopting them out together. I guess I'll have to separate them."

"Well," Roe said, petting the piggies. "I wouldn't want them to be separated."

"Fergie here likes them too," Mack said, taking the white-and-brown one and setting it next to Fergie. "Look, he's not even trying to eat it."

Roe arched a brow. "I'm not sure that means that he likes them."

Fergie whined and licked the guinea pig's head.

"Okay, that was cute." Roe chuckled. "I guess we have two guinea pigs now."

Doc Grover stood and grinned. "Wonderful. I'll get their cage and food from the car. They're actually litter trained, if you can believe it."

"Okay?" Roe patted the piggy on his shoulder and watched Doc Grover practically skip out the door. "Ian, I think we just got played."

"I warned you." Mack shrugged and pet Fergie and the other piggy. "You should name this one Pepper and that one Carrot. Benji would like that."

"You are no help at all." Roe laughed and leaned back in the comfortable chair. Mmrr watched them from under the couch. They would have to keep an eye on her and the guinea pigs until they knew how she would react.

"Doc does this all the time." Mack laughed. "The only reason I've escaped being conned into a pet is because I'm at the station so much. I have a feeling that will change. Next thing you know, he'll say Mmrr needs a new friend since Fergie and the guinea pigs are all friends."

Roe chuckled. "Don't tell him this, but I love it. Doc Grover seems really nice, and he clearly loves animals. Anyone who takes the time to find strays the perfect home is deserving of a little leniency."

"I will definitely not tell him that." Mack shuddered. "Remind me to introduce you to Cain's brother, Carter. He literally can't say no to Doc. Now, he has a barn full of animals."

Roe yawned and pulled Carrot off his shoulder and to his chest. "Do you think this guinea pig will poop on me if I try to take a nap with it?"

"Probably."

"I'm too late," Wally said, coming into the room. He

chuckled as he moved to kneel next to Roe's chair. "Mack's vet friend already got you."

Roe smiled sleepily. "Yep. Meet Carrot and Pepper."

"Cute." Wally smirked and shook his head. "I had a guinea pig when I was a kid. Damn thing was the most demanding fuzzy potato I've ever seen."

"Hey, Sheriff, can we come in?" someone asked from the front door.

Wally's eyes narrowed, and he stood quickly.

"Friend, not foe," Mack said, patting Wally's shoulder as he passed him. "Come on in, Harper."

"Your friend with the table?" Wally asked, still hyperaware of the two strangers coming inside. One was a young man with brown hair, and the other was an older man who was maybe in his late sixties or early seventies. They carried a cute cedar table between them.

"This is Harper Wilson and his grandpa, Gerald." Mack moved to help them with the table.

"Everyone calls me Gramps," the older man said, grinning. He let Mack take his side of the table and sat down across from Roe. "How are you, Roe? Cain told me you've been through a lot."

Roe pressed his lips together and struggled to not start crying. The man reminded him of his omega grandfather, Ben. He had a very steady and gentle presence that made Roe want to tell him all his troubles.

"I'm fine," he managed to say in a small voice.

Gramps gave him a long look. "Fine?"

Roe's bottom lip trembled, and he widened his eyes, struggling to keep his composure. "Really. Just fine."

The man's knowing blue eyes were too much.

"Okay, I'm not fine." Roe groaned and covered his face. "This has been a nightmare."

The seat sank beside him, and Gramps wrapped an arm

around his shoulders. "I would think so. That ex of yours is a right piece of work."

"It's mostly his new husband, I think." Roe wiped his eyes and smiled wanly. "At least, Gabriel *seems* to be the one doing everything, but James supports him."

"Cain and his people will take care of it." Gramps patted his knee. "If any of them show up here in town, I know the best places to bury the bodies."

The words should have alarmed Roe, but he was sure Gramps was joking. Well, he was at least 40 percent sure he was joking.

"Don't talk about burying bodies when I can hear you, Gerald!" Mack shouted from the sunroom.

Gramps snorted. "I watched that man fall on his face running up a slide when he was a boy. Six times in a row. I'm not worried about him."

Roe chuckled. It was hard to imagine the steady and competent man doing something so silly. It was also fascinating. "Tell me more."

"Well, there was the time he got chased through town by a chicken. That was only a few months ago, though."

Roe laughed so hard he almost fell off the couch.

"To be fair, that chicken was a mean one, but it sure was a lot smaller than him," Gramps said with a chuckle. "Then, there was the time Violet Timberline thought he was a peeping tom. It was his first year as a police officer. She called in saying there was a shady character hanging around her house, and he answered the call. When she saw him skulking around, she sprayed him with the hose until he looked like a drowned cat. The poor woman really needed new glasses, but she refused to go to the new eye doctor in town until she knew him better."

Roe rolled with laughter, wiggling in his seat.

"Damn it, Gerald." Mack stood in front of them, scowling with his arms crossed.

Gramps gave him an innocent look. "What's the problem, Sheriff?"

Mack growled and threw himself into the chair nearby. "You Wilsons are gonna be the death of me. Between the pranks your grandkids play on one another and the general silliness of the whole family, I should put you all in jail."

"Bah," Gramps scoffed. "All you'd have to do then is write traffic tickets. We make life more interesting."

AFTER HARPER AND GRAMPS LEFT, Roe found himself secluded in his cute new, sunny studio. The work table and chair were absolutely stunning. Harper had made them himself, and Roe fully planned to beg the craftsman to work with him on the custom wooden frames he enjoyed making. Roe wasn't nearly as talented with wood as Harper was, and ideas swirled in his head of ways to integrate Harper's work with his own.

While Roe had the skills to be a traditional oil and canvas artist, he preferred mixed media art, which allowed him to use anything from paper or sculptures to beads and rocks. He almost felt sorry for Harper, but the young man was too talented to ignore.

Roe grabbed his sketchbook and pencils before awkwardly lowering himself onto the overstuffed chair and ottoman Mack had arranged for him in the corner of the studio. He lost himself in drawing, imagining beautiful pieces built of wood and metal surrounding painted canvases textured with leaves and pressed flowers. Wood was earthy and natural, just begging to be paired with sage or wine-red paint.

At some point, a cup of tea and a sandwich appeared on the small table beside him. A post-it told him the kids were home and watching a movie upstairs. Roe smiled and ate as he fleshed out the design that appealed to him the most—an oak shadow box carved to appear as if it was peeled open to reveal a textured painting of sage, cream, and pale blue. Small wooden acorns, gold filigree leaves, a soft purple tulip. Mischievous eyes on a sweet face with a crooked grin. A little faun, curled into his hiding spot.

Hours later, Roe finally looked up, his muscles stiff and aching from remaining locked in place. Another cup of tea sat on the side table, and the lunch dishes were gone. Mack. The man was too damn sweet to be single, that was for sure. James had mocked Roe constantly about getting lost in his *trivial* work. Mack had been more supportive in one day than James had been throughout their entire marriage.

He slowly got to his feet, wincing as his bruises reminded him that he had almost died three days ago. Wally sat in a chair right outside the studio reading a book. Roe patted his shoulder as he walked by.

The teacup was warm in his hand as he wandered through the quiet house. His phone said it was just after seven. Fergie slept on his dog bed with Carrot cuddled against his side. Mmrr was sprawled inside the large open guinea pig cage licking Pepper. The guinea pig's wet hair stuck up, but she didn't seem concerned about the cat. Mmrr had never been one to hunt rodents. Instead, she mostly enjoyed lounging, so Roe decided to take his cue from Pepper.

A soft giggle came from the kitchen.

Roe followed the sound and stopped in the entry. Pizza boxes covered the counters, and the delicious smell made his stomach growl. Mack and the kids were gathered around the table with a familiar gameboard laid out in front of them.

Benji sat on Mack's lap, clearly providing his expert help on *Munchkin*, the family's favorite game.

"Okay, I can totally take a potted plant," Daphne said, grinning. "I have fifteen strength against its one. No one can mess this up for me. I *will* get to level nine."

"Oh, my dearest sister," Tris said, smirking, "How wrong you are. I have three cards to play here to increase that potted plant's power to sixteen."

He laid them on the table, crowing with joy.

Daphne groaned. "Seriously? I can't even take a potted plant?"

"Should we help, Benji?" Mack asked.

The little boy scrunched up his face, thinking hard. "Daffy makes cookies."

Tris scowled. "I'll make you cookies if you don't help her, Benji."

"Tris burn cookies." Benji shook his head, looking immensely sad. "Poor cookies."

Mack snickered. "That decides it. Add our twenty-six strength to her fifteen."

Daphne pumped her fist while Tris groaned, flopping back in his seat.

"I hope you draw the plutonium dragon on your next turn," Tris said, glaring at Daphne. "I'm winning this time, darn it."

Roe shook his head and started looking through the cabinets. It appeared cookies were needed to keep the peace.

# CHAPTER 5

*L*ater that evening, after the kids were in bed and Wally was doing one last patrol of the property, Mack looked through Roe's sketchbook. The man was talented and had an intriguing imagination.

"This is beautiful," Mack said, shaking his head in awe. "I can almost guarantee that Harper will enjoy helping create it."

Roe lounged back in the chair Mack had dug out of the attic, his long fingers wrapped around a mug of chamomile tea.

A sweet, slightly shy smile lit Roe from the inside out. "Thank you for today. It's been a while since I've been that into my art. I'm glad I got to finish the sketch. Harper is about to become my new best friend. That's just how it's going to be."

Mack snorted a laugh and sat on the ottoman next to Roe's feet. "I think he'll enjoy that—or at least tolerate it."

Roe chuckled for a moment and then settled back in his chair with a contented sigh. "This is the most relaxed I've been in two years. That's nuts, right?"

"Not at all." Mack fought back a scowl as he thought of Roe's ex. "Have James and Gabriel been like this since the divorce?"

Roe shook his head. "Nope. At first, everything was okay. James got what he wanted: the company. He and Gabriel married as soon as the divorce was final, and I thought I'd never hear from them again. That should have been it. Hell, James kept my name, so he's even a Dorsey running Dorsey Investments."

"I'm sorry you lost the family business."

"It's not so bad." Roe's eyes grew soft. "I never wanted to work there. Grandpa Ben encouraged me to focus on my art. All I ever wanted were children and my art. My parents and Grandpa Roland understood. They loved the business, but it was because they built it together. Family was always the priority."

"That sounds about right." Mack nodded. "Darren and I had that focus too. Our parents didn't, for one reason or another, but we wanted to build our family with that principle as a foundation. Family and unconditional love."

A slightly calloused hand came to rest on top of his own. "How long has he been gone?"

"Almost fifteen years now." Mack leaned forward, bracing his arms on his knees. "He got sick, cancer. One day he seemed good, and a few weeks later, he was gone."

Roe squeezed Mack's hand. "Tell me about him?"

Mack grinned. "He was a pistol. Adventurous and wild, but loyal to a fault. Fierce and protective. He knew how to love with every bit of his heart."

"I wish I could have met him," Roe said softly. "I'd beg him to teach me that whole heart thing."

"You have that down already."

Roe arched a brow. "Do I?"

Mack nodded. "I've seen you with your kids. You love them fiercely."

"That's easy." Roe's nose wrinkled. "Trusting another adult enough to love them like that? Too scary."

Mack covered their linked hands with his free one. "It's the scariest damn thing in the world, but when it works? It's the most beautiful experience you'll ever have."

Roe looked thoughtful for a moment. "I don't know if I can do that. I loved James when we first married. Well, I loved who I thought James was. After the first few months, he became a different person. When anyone else was around, he was still loving and supportive, but if we were alone, he basically just ignored me."

"What did your grandfathers say?"

"Grandpa Roland thought I was exaggerating." Roe made a face. "He adored James. Grandpa Ben saw right through him, though. He was convinced James only pursued me because he wanted in the company. By then, I was pregnant with Tris, and that made me so happy. Happy enough that I didn't mind being ignored by my husband."

"Tris is a good kid." Mack remembered how happy he'd been when Darren had gotten pregnant. They hadn't been trying, but they hadn't been *not* trying either. Darren was a park ranger and didn't want to miss too much work. Mack had just been made a deputy, and he hadn't wanted to jeopardize that either, but babies had a way of changing things. By the time Lacey arrived, neither of them had wanted to leave her side for a single second.

"Then, a few years later, Daphne came along," Roe said, smiling happily. "Those two made putting up with James worth everything."

"Lacey sure changed things when she came along," Mack said, chuckling. "Before her, we never really thought about kids. We had our work, and we loved traveling. Darren and I would go camping up in Canada at least twice a month. We went all over the country and even made it to the Philippines one year."

Roe laughed. "How did that work with Lacey?"

"Oh, we still went camping," Mack said, wincing. "We just went a lot better prepared."

"I bet." Roe giggled. "Tris was such a high-maintenance baby. He would have perished without his homemade fresh organic butternut squash. Well, at least he thought he would."

Mack laughed, picturing a tiny Tris wailing because he had to eat regular baby food. "I'd have liked to see that."

"What about when Lacey was older?" Roe asked, stifling his giggles.

"The traveling slowed down, but we got to go to a few places with her. Everything costs more with a kid. It didn't matter though. Our wanderlust was never the same. I would rather go to the bookstore with her than travel to Italy without her."

"Oh, I love that." Roe pretended to swoon. "Such a good papa."

Mack preened at the compliment. "Lacey doesn't complain."

"Do you think we can meet her?" Roe bit his lip once the words were out, clearly second-guessing himself. "Not that we have to or anything. I know we're imposing on you as it is."

Mack scowled. "Hey now. We're friends. I'd love to introduce you to Lacey and her lady love. She'll talk your ear off about their upcoming wedding, but she and Renee are lovely women. You'll like them."

"I don't doubt it," Roe said. "Maybe they can meet Daphne too. I worry sometimes that she spends so much time with the boys. She doesn't have many girlfriends. Lord, she hates the school she went to. Said everyone was too pretentious."

"Are you going to sign up for school here?" Mack asked, already mentally listing the teens he knew. If Daphne needed girlfriends, he'd find her some.

"I think so. Tris is headed to Harvard in a few weeks, so it will just be Daphne. I might see if there's a good daycare in the area for Benji, but I'm not too worried about that. He's my surprise baby, so I'm especially enjoying him while he's cuddly."

"As it should be." Mack nodded, remembering those precious years with Lacey. "If you do decide on daycare, we have a good one in town. There are a few kids his age who go, and I can introduce him anytime you want. Ms. Ines runs it out of her home, and I know Min goes."

When Benji and the others got home from the bookstore, the little boy had been very excited to tell Mack about his new friend, Min. They were about the same age and had bonded quickly. Mack knew Min's parents and other siblings. They were all friends of the Wilsons. Everything seemed to come back to that family, damn it.

"I don't know if I'll be able to keep him away then," Roe said dryly. "I've never seen Benji that excited about meeting someone."

"At least you'll have more time for your art," Mack said with a laugh.

"I wish I could have another baby." Roe smiled wistfully. "I always wanted a big family. Three kids should really be six, right?"

Mack winced and reached up to feel Roe's forehead. "You're not feverish, but you must be sick. Why else would you say something like that?"

Roe smacked at his hand with a laugh. "Now you sound like Cain. He wants to move here, you know. He won't admit it, but he misses his family and wants to be closer. I think if I wasn't in trouble, he'd have put Jasper in charge and set up an office here."

"You two are good friends, right?" Mack didn't like the dark *something* wiggling around in his gut at the thought of Cain and Roe together.

"He's my official best friend." Roe nodded firmly. "My BFF. My brother by another. My best bro bud."

"How would you feel if he moved here?"

Roe mused on it for a moment. "I'd talk to the kids about moving here permanently. There's nothing in Georgia for me anymore. Even my grandparents' home doesn't feel like home, and my family's gone now. Grandpa Ben passed about six years ago, and Grandpa Roland went quickly after him. My parents died in a car crash right before everything blew up with James. All my previous friends dropped me like a hot potato after the divorce."

Mack pictured Roe and the kids living in town. Benji would likely be joined at the hip with Min and the other Wilson littles. Daphne would fit right in with a couple of teens he knew. Tris would have a welcoming home to come to on school breaks. Most importantly of all, Mack knew Roe would make more friends here in town. He didn't think anyone could possibly resist Roe's sweet smile and kind nature. Mack sure couldn't.

"I think I need to have a talk with Cain's parents." Mack took Roe's empty teacup and helped the other man to his feet. "It's time all the Bensons lived in Hobson Hills."

THE NEXT MORNING brought in a summer thunderstorm. Mack was unusually reluctant to go into work. Breakfast with Roe and the kids had been fun. By the time he left, Roe and Benji were fingerpainting, Daphne was cuddling with

Fergie and the guinea pigs, and Tris was video chatting with his friends.

Wally smirked from where he stood, leaning against the wall near the door. "With the way you drag your feet, I'd think you don't trust me to keep them safe, except I see the way your eyes linger on Roe."

Mack's face warmed as he blushed. "Don't be ridiculous. I'm too old for that, and Roe could do a lot better than me."

Wally's eyes softened. "What about what he thinks? You don't give yourself enough credit, Mack. I'm ten years younger than Roe, and I'd be after you in a heartbeat if I thought it would do any good. There's nothing hotter than a silver fox."

Mack almost choked on his own spit, and Wally laughed at his reaction.

"I'm going to work before the bullshit gets any deeper." Mack shook his head and left the house in a hurry. He was sure his face was beet red.

The morning passed quickly with two drug-related arrests and a few personnel meetings. Someone was stealing from an outdoor vending machine at a convenience store in town. It always happened after closing hours, so they made a plan to keep watch until they caught them.

After lunch, Mack visited with a few of the older citizens in town. Ms. Margaret lived in a small older neighborhood at the edge of town. She didn't have children of her own, and her sister was all the way in Portland. A few of the kids in the neighborhood did chores for her like weeding and keeping the tiny yard around her home mowed, but Mack liked to help out when he had the time.

"It shouldn't take me long to fix these steps, ma'am." Mack surveyed the wobbly steps leading to her front porch. "I have a few pieces of wood in the back of my car that should work."

"Thank you, sweetheart." Ms. Margaret pulled her shawl

tighter around her thin shoulders. "Birdie's going to paint the porch for me next week, but she didn't know how to fix the steps."

The teenager had just turned fourteen and had sprouted up like a weed during the summer. She stood next to him, shuffling from foot to foot, as she looked over the steps. She had warm-brown skin, jean shorts with a few trendy holes in them, and a too-big T-shirt that hung off one shoulder. She kept her long black hair in box braids pulled into a neat little bun on the top of her head.

Birdie's parents worked long hours, so she and the other Harris kids spent a lot of time with Ms. Margaret. They were a tight-knit family and very nice. *She'd make a good friend*, he thought.

Birdie narrowed her eyes. "Why are you looking at me like that? I'm gonna watch you build the steps so I can repair it next time."

"I was just thinking," Mack said, shaking his head. "I have a friend with a daughter your age. She's new to town. Think you might like to meet her?"

"Think she might like to help paint a porch?" Birdie asked with a smirk.

Mack snorted a laugh. "If it got her out of the house and away from her brothers, she just might."

"I feel that in my soul." Birdie patted her heart. "Right here."

"I'll ask her and bring her by next week." Mack turned toward his car. "I'll use the skill saw, but you can nail the boards together."

"Gotcha." Birdie followed behind him.

"I'll make you two some lemonade," Ms. Margaret said, smiling wide. "You'll have earned it."

# CHAPTER 6

Two weeks later, Roe isolated himself in his studio and worked on a new sketch. Harper was working on their shadow box, and Roe had a damn image in his head that wouldn't go away. When he closed his eyes, all he could see was Mack sitting across from him with that smile on his face. The slightly crooked one that meant he was amused, but trying not to show it. Crinkles at the corner of his blue eyes. A strong jaw begging to be kissed. Ears that poked out a little too much. Dark hair sprinkled liberally with silver and gray.

Roe groaned and knocked his head against his table a couple times. *Wide shoulders that can carry the whole world*, he thought.

Mack had managed to help Roe's family so much in such a short time. Tris was looking forward to college again, and Daphne and Benji both had wonderful best friends. The man made Roe feel something that he hadn't felt in a very long time. Bravery. He wanted Mack as his own. *His* partner, *his* lover, *his* friend.

Roe took a long breath and slowly released it, easing his

panic. The idea of trusting someone with his heart again was frightening.

"Uh, is this a bad time?" Harper asked from the door with Wally looming behind him.

Roe slammed his sketchbook shut and stumbled to his feet. "Hey. I didn't know you were coming by today."

"My husband wanted to meet—"

"Hi," a man said, pushing past Wally and Harper. "I'm Grey, Harper's omega."

Grey was a cute young man with golden-brown skin and green eyes. "Our kids are with my abuela, so a few of my friends are getting together at Honey Buns. Harper said your kids are all with friends right now, so you can come."

"Um," Roe searched for a way to politely decline. Daphne and Birdie had gone to a movie, Tris was shopping for his dorm room with Gramps, and Benji was at Min's house. Roe really needed to work out the mess in his head. Usually, that meant jogging or escaping into his art, but he couldn't jog with his ankle, and he'd already filled one sketchpad up with pictures of Mack. Plus, he hadn't been out of the house in over two weeks.

Grey bounced on the tips of his feet. "Zoe makes the absolute best donuts. You really need to try them."

"Donuts, huh?" Roe thought for a moment. "With chocolate frosting?"

"Of course."

"Okay." Roe patted his pockets. "I'll grab my wallet."

"Maybe change your shirt," Wally suggested.

Roe looked down. He'd worn this T-shirt for the past three days, and you could tell. Paint and glue stained it, and it had its own *unique* odor.

"Good idea." He headed toward the stairs.

"Maybe take a shower," Grey said, following him. "I'll play with those guinea pigs while I wait. They are so cute."

Fergie followed Roe upstairs and watched over him as he showered, dressed, and pulled on loose cargo shorts and his old Savannah College of Art and Design T-shirt with SCAD in big letters below their mascot, a bee.

By the time he was back downstairs, Roe was feeling a little more human. Grey set Carrot back down, and Fergie went to check that his guinea pigs were all right.

"Where did Harper go?" Roe asked. Wally stood at the window, but he didn't see Harper anywhere.

"He had some errands to run." Grey stood and linked his arm in Roe's. "Do you want to walk? You're wearing a boot, but it's just a couple of blocks."

"That would be nice." Roe looked at Wally uncertainly. He didn't know the protocol for bringing your body-guard/friend along on an outing.

"Oh, Wally here is good to go," Grey said, smiling at the large man. "My friends will like him too, and we may share some donuts with him."

"Maybe," Roe agreed, fighting a smile.

"We can bring Fergie too," Wally said. "The kids say there are outdoor tables."

Fergie ran over, his nubby tail wagging, when he heard his name. A few minutes later, they were out the door.

It was warm but not nearly as sweltering as Roe was used to. The town was cute; it had large green trees, flowering shrubs, and neat sidewalks. Mack's neighborhood of family homes transitioned into lovely townhouses a block over.

"That's Abuela's house," Grey said, pointing at a bright-blue door. "She's basically everyone's abuela, so if you need a babysitter, just ask. She loves kids and is basically a daycare. Oh, that's where Jackson and Juan live." He pointed at the house next to his abuela's. "Jackson is Min's older brother. He spends a lot of time there, and since he's now besties with your youngest, you'll probably find your way there soon."

They walked slowly, and Grey pointed out the sights along the way: the post office, the best store for fresh produce, and the open lot where the farmers' market gathered on weekends.

By the time they reached Honey Buns, Roe felt like he'd lived there forever.

The bakery was cute with bright designs on the front window and iron patio tables out front with colorful umbrellas. Two tables were pushed together to seat a group of five with a few more empty seats.

"That's us." Grey pointed toward the table and tugged Roe with him. "Hey, everyone. I have two new members to introduce. Roe and Wally."

"Members?" Roe asked, sharing a baffled look with Wally.

A young blond man leaned forward with a smirk. "Didn't you know? This is a meeting of the Hot Mess Club."

"What now?" Roe arched a brow. "*I* know I'm a hot mess, but how do you all know?"

"We're all hot messes here," an alpha with a rabbit strapped across his chest in a baby carrier said.

"That's Caden," Grey said, pointing to the man with the rabbit. "Huckleberry is his rabbit."

"Cain's brother?" Roe asked.

Caden nodded and smiled shyly.

"I'm Justin," the blond said. "I didn't bring a rabbit with me because I'm a normal person."

Fergie whined and went to sniff Caden's shoe, clearly wanting to say hello to the rabbit. Caden knelt down and introduced the two.

"I'm Abel," another blond said with a wide smile. "I am also normal, but if I had a rabbit that wanted to come along with me, I would bring one everywhere."

"Not normal," Justin said, rolling his eyes.

Grey ignored them and pointed at an older, Hispanic

omega. "This is Eduardo. He's from Arizona and is our newest member."

The older man smiled sweetly. "It's nice to meet you, gentlemen."

"And this is Fawn," Grey finished, waving to the only woman at the table. The blonde was about his age and well put together in designer clothing. She really did look familiar.

"Fawn," Roe mused, thinking. "Do I know you?"

"Cook Enterprises," she said, waving him into a chair. "My ex-husband's family ran it."

"Oh yeah," he said, happy to be off his ankle. "I read about . . . Never mind. This is Wally, he's my bodyguard."

"Nice topic change," Fawn said, laughing. "It's all right, though. Everyone knows my ex-husband was a horrible man. That's old news. Tell us why the beloved grandson of Roland and Ben Dorsey needs a bodyguard."

"Explain your hot-mess-ness." Abel leaned forward. "Give us all the details."

"I'll get those donuts," Grey said, wiggling happily. "And coffee."

"Earl Grey tea for me and a mocha latte for Wally," Roe said, patting his bodyguard's arm. "Now, where to start?"

FOUR HOURS and three dozen donuts later, Roe knew everything juicy about each of the others at the table—even Wally—and they knew everything about him. He wasn't alone in his hot-mess-ness at all. The others had dealt with their fair share of trouble.

"I'm just saying," Abel muttered, "if James and Gabriel were to *accidentally* fall in a volcano, would anyone really notice?"

"Forget about that," Justin said, elbowing Abel in the side. "Tell me more about these sketches of the sheriff. Are they nude? Did he model for you? Can you talk him into modeling for you?"

"I think I need to text your husband about this obsession you have with his boss," Caden said, snorting a laugh. Justin was married to Mack's deputy, Tanner.

"Are you kidding me?" Justin said, giving a short bark of laughter. "Tanner would insist on seeing the sketches. Sheriff McKenzie is a fine looking man."

"Silver fox," Wally agreed, playing with the spoon in his teacup.

Roe pressed his hands to his warm cheeks. "I think I'd prefer to talk about almost dying."

"Cain will take care of that," Caden said. "Tell Justin what the sheriff looks like with his shirt off before he combusts."

Eduardo tsked. "You boys leave Roe alone. Clearly, he has only just realized his little crush on the sheriff. Maybe you could make a move at the summer festival. It's this weekend. Wouldn't that be lovely? Very small-town romance."

"Nope. That's way too silly." Fawn leaned her chin on her fist and sipped at her tea. "What would he do? Go on the Ferris wheel with him and profuse his love? Blah! Besides, the longer he thinks about it, the more doubts he'll have. Sometimes you just have to act, not think."

"Your body should act all over Sheriff McKenzie's body," Abel said, nodding sagely. "It's the logical thing to do."

"You are all bad influences." Roe glared at them. "You'd have me strip him naked at the front door, wouldn't you?"

Fawn shrugged. "Well, that's one idea, I suppose. Perhaps make sure the kids aren't home first. Oh, and Wally may need to check the cameras. You certainly don't want a sex tape leaked to the media."

~

LATER THAT EVENING, Roe snuggled on the sofa with Benji as they watched *Frozen* for the thirtieth time. Birdie and Daphne were having a sleepover. They had shut themselves away in her attic room with snacks. Tris was video chatting with some of his friends—*again*—even though he would be headed to school in less than a week.

Roe hugged Benji closer, already missing Tris.

"Is Benji your emotional support baby?" Mack asked, sitting down. "You look like your heart is breaking."

"Tris is eighteen." Roe made a face. "His brain isn't even fully developed yet. Why can't he just stay with me forever? Is that too much to ask?"

Mack chuckled. "You know the answer to that. I hate to be the one to tell you, but it doesn't get any easier. Children become adults, but they'll always be your children. I'm still wrapping my head around Lacey getting married."

"She's going to be at the festival tomorrow, right?"

Mack nodded. "She wants to meet you all. Renee will be there too."

Roe snuffled the top of Benji's head. The more attracted he grew to Mack, the more he worried about meeting Lacey. She was the center of Mack's world. What if she didn't like Roe or the kids?

"Cain called today," Mack said, leaning back.

Roe groaned. "I don't want to think about that right now. It's a mess."

"That it is." Mack nudged Roe's shoulder with his own. "I thought we caught the vending machine thief last night. Did I tell you about that?"

"No, what happened?" Roe asked. Mack had worked late last night, and they hadn't really had a chance to talk. He was becoming addicted to their talks.

"We had everything arranged perfectly. It was after midnight, and a car pulled into the gas station. It's closed, so there's no reason for it to be there, right? Anyway, the car pulls in and parks, but no one gets out. Three squad cars pull in and block each of the exits, and I rush up, ready to read the thief his rights and cuff him. Tanner and Parker are right behind me like good little deputies."

"Oh my goodness." Roe leaned closer.

"The window rolls down, and it's Yeo, the bookstore owner. He's stuffing his face with tacos from the fast-food place down the street. He's a little over four months pregnant and wanted a snack. Didn't want to make a mess in the car, but also didn't want to wait until he got home."

Roe laughed hard, falling into Mack's side. "That's Caden's husband, right? Why didn't he just make Caden go get them?"

Mack sighed. "Who knows? Sometimes, I think the Wilsons and the Wilson adjacents live to make my job harder."

"At least he wasn't the vending machine thief. Imagine having to deal with the Bensons over that." Roe giggled again and grabbed his phone to text Cain. "I have to tell Cain his brother-in-law almost got arrested for eating tacos." He gasped as a thought came to him. "Wait, am I Wilson adjacent since Cain is my best friend?"

"No, don't say that," Mack groaned and covered his face. "You can't be Wilson adjacent. You just can't."

Roe snorted and nudged his side. "Do you want to hold Benji? He'll make you feel better."

Mack pulled the little boy into his lap. "Hi'ya, Benji."

Benji snuggled into him, eyes transfixed on the screen. He loved the damn snowman in the movie more than anything.

Roe pulled his sketchbook from the table and started a new drawing. The relaxed lines of Mack's handsome face and a transfixed Benji made for the perfect inspiration. Moments like this were too precious. He'd just have to figure out how to hide his attraction from the man who was becoming so important to him. He didn't want to lose his Ian.

~

HOBSON HILLS'S Summer festival was held in the center of town. Booths of games lined the walkway, and food trucks gathered in one corner. A few small kiddie rides, a petting zoo, and a small stage took up the rest of the space. At the moment, a live band played music on the stage, but there were several events scheduled for the weekend.

"Why did I have to go meet the hot messes?" Roe asked, growling under his breath. "Now all I can think about is riding on the stupid Ferris wheel with Ian."

Wally snickered. "The festival doesn't even have a Ferris wheel."

Roe pinched his side, scowling when he only got muscle. "Hush you. You're absolutely no help."

He watched Mack throw a dart at a balloon trying to win prizes for Benji and Daphne while Tris cheered him on. The handsome man wore his faded jeans and a tight, thin black shirt. Roe's mouth did *not* water. It was all Fergie's fault. He was allergic to his dog. That's all.

Fergie grinned up at him, tongue hanging out. The guinea pigs were quite comfortable in their new stroller, happy as could be as they munched on some green leaf lettuce. Mmrr, of course, insisted on staying home. She was a loner.

"I can't believe you brought the guinea pigs," Wally murmured, scanning the small crowd.

"When in Hobson Hills," Roe said with a shrug. Caden

carried his rabbit around everywhere, so Roe thought it was only right that he buy a stroller for the guinea pigs. They liked getting out in the sunshine and seeing the sights.

A lovely tall blonde woman ran past them and hugged Mack tightly. A shorter, pretty brown-skinned woman followed behind her, joining the hug.

"Lacey McKenzie and Renee Donahue," Wally said with a grunt. "Both age twenty-seven. Best friends since elementary school, started dating in college, and are now engaged to be married August 26th. Both have decent credit scores and good jobs, though Donahue does have a few too many credit cards. They live together across town from Mack, and they are taking the classes to become foster parents."

"You ran a background check on Ian's daughter?" Roe frowned. "Why would you do that?"

Wally shrugged. "I run checks on everyone. Everyone has secrets, and you never know when some random bit of information will come in handy. For example, Cain's buying a house near his parents here in Hobson Hills but hasn't told anyone yet. I know all kinds of useful information."

"To do what?" Roe asked, rolling his eyes. "Take over the world?"

"Keep you safe." Wally slung an arm around him and steered them toward the others. "Now, stop procrastinating and meet Mack's daughter. You know you want to."

"You don't know me," Roe mumbled, pouting.

"No one knows, but you make a good living selling your art through two galleries—one in New York and the other in Savannah—using an alias. You're a registered foster parent in Georgia and have been thinking about adopting. However, you want to wait until Benji is a little older. You've been researching realtors back in Georgia because you're thinking of selling the house and moving here. You kind of want a pet rabbit, but you don't want to share it with the kids. You have a big ol' crush on a silver fox sheriff and are nervous about meeting his daughter."

"I hate you," Roe said, no heat in his voice.

"Oh, and your favorite color is purple, and you sleep sprawled out diagonally across your bed." Wally grinned. "Shall I go on?"

"Privacy-invading bodyguards are very irritating." Roe sniffed, nose in the air. "Just so you know."

Mack's hug with his daughter and soon to be daughter-in-law was just ending when Roe and Wally reached them. It was only then that Roe noticed Benji had wiggled his way into the hug, clinging to Mack's legs possessively.

"This must be Benji," Renee said, kneeling down beside Roe's son. "I hear you're having a lot of fun with Mack."

Benji nodded furiously. "Macky friend. We parsers."

"Partners," Daphne absentmindedly corrected him, eyeing a fluffy purple teddy bear.

"Hi," Roe said, holding out his hand to Lacey. "I'm Roe, and these are my kids, Tris, Daphne, and Benji."

Lacey smiled hesitantly but then quickly shook his hand. "I'm Lacey, and this is Renee."

"Baby girl," Benji said, patting Lacey's leg.

Mack laughed. "Right, buddy. She's my baby girl." He picked Benji up and settled him on his hip. "Lacey, Tris here is planning on studying business at Harvard. Do you have any advice for him?"

Lacey whistled. "Harvard, huh?"

Tris flushed and ducked his head. "Yeah. My grandpa went there too."

"Nice," she said, moving to stand beside him. "I would suggest double majoring in finance or economics too. It'll make you more marketable."

The two started chatting, and Renee took Mack's leftover darts. "You want that bear, Daphne?"

Daphne nodded. "My friend Birdie's little sister loves purple. I want to give it to her."

"I gotcha, girl. Let's win this bear." Renee's eyes narrowed, and she studied the board of balloons.

"I think they've stolen your kids," Mack said, sighing as he watched Lacey and Tris wander toward the food trucks as Renee hit three balloons in a row, making Daphne cheer.

"Still got one left," Roe said, tickling Benji.

"Sheriff McKenzie, look at you," a young man said, sliding in between Mack and Roe. "Oh, that's just the cutest little baby."

With blond hair and bright-blue eyes, the man was stunning. He looked vaguely familiar, but Roe couldn't place him.

"Hey, Griff." Mack smiled down at the young man. "Meet Benji."

Griff practically cooed, but he wasn't looking at Benji. He was staring adoringly at Mack. "I just love a handsome man with a baby."

Roe scowled, his gut churning unpleasantly.

"Oh my, is that our hunky sheriff?" another man asked, moving to stand next to Griff. Three more young men followed, gathering around them and unsubtly shoving Roe further away.

"I never noticed how blue your eyes are, Sheriff," a dark-haired man said, smiling sweetly.

"Do you work out every day?" another asked. "Parker told me the station has a small workout area, and your muscles are so firm." He squeezed Mack's arm. "Feel his muscles, Nico. Aren't they firm?"

"They're sooo firm, Ernie." Nico fanned himself.

Mack looked puzzled, but he shrugged off their

comments. Roe, however, wasn't at all confused. He *knew* what kind of men these were. They were uniform groupies, or whatever they called them. They probably followed Mack around, hoping to get his attention.

"Sleazy," he muttered, crossing his arms across his chest. If Mack wasn't careful, he'd find himself in a compromising position.

Roe ignored the little voice in his head that was laughing its ass off at his reaction. It may sound a bit Victorian, but Mack held an important position in town and needed to be aware of his reputation. Sleazy men could cause a lot of problems, and really, if Roe could help even a little, he would. It was his civic duty.

"Such a cute baby," Nico said, practically whimpering as he tucked himself in against Mack's side.

Mack nodded agreeably. "Roe said Benji looks just like his great-grandpa Ben. Freckles and all."

Roe stomped his foot and growled. Nico wasn't interested in Roe's baby's freckles. He wanted Mack's body, damn it. Wally snickered, but Roe ignored him.

"Enough of this shit." He shoved his way through the throng of hussies and pried Nico from Mack's side to take his place. "Honey, I'm ready for the food trucks. How about you?"

Mack looked down at him, head cocked to the side. "Huh?"

Obviously, Roe's friend wasn't very observative. Hopefully he was better at spotting crime. "Darling," Roe said, drawing out the word. "Food trucks. Now."

"Um, okay?" Mack looked at Benji as if the toddler could explain what was happening. Benji grinned and kissed his cheek.

*Good idea*, Roe thought and quickly leaned up and pressed his lips to Mack's. The instant they touched, he promptly forgot that he was only doing this to protect Mack from uniform groupies. The sounds of the crowd and the pop of the balloons faded away. Blood rushed to his head, and all he could hear was his own quickening heartbeat. All he could smell was the warm pine scent of Mack's cologne mixing with his natural smell. Heaven.

His eyes closed as heat rushed through him, and he melted against Mack. Wrapping one arm around his neck and settling one hand on the back of his head, his fingers tangled with his soft, short hair. His lips were softer than Roe thought they would be, and his jaw was a little bristly.

Mack tasted sweet, like cotton candy and soda. All of Roe's guilty pleasures combined. His mouth opened against Roe's, and he deepened the kiss, delving into him, soaking up every heated sensation he could.

What seemed like hours passed as Roe learned the feel and taste of Mack's kiss. He was sure he would be happy to stand there all night long, but Benji's soft pats against his cheek brought him straight back to reality.

Roe pulled away, breaking the kiss with a low moan. Mack watched him in a daze, eyes full of confused heat.

Roe cleared his throat and glared at the giggling men around them. "There, see. He's taken. Go find someone else to shamelessly flirt with."

"Huh?" Mack tilted his head again, eyes still on Roe.

"They're shameless," Roe said, waving at the laughing men. "All shameless."

"You heard him, men. Get!" Abel appeared beside Roe and started dispersing the crowd. "Go away, you shameless hussies. No sheriff for you."

Each of the young men laughed, clearly not offended.

Roe frowned, noticing for the first time that the rest of the Hot Mess Club stood nearby. Caden was recording them with his phone while Fawn, Justin, and Grey laughed. Eduardo gave him a sympathetic look.

Realization dawned slowly, and he turned to slap Abel's arm. "You set me up."

"What?" Abel asked, eyes comically large. "Would we do that? Are these shameless hussies our family and friends? Do we now owe them ten dollars each?"

"Yes, you do." Nico elbowed Abel's side. "Ernie said he didn't need ten dollars. He figures this will annoy Lacey, so he was happy to flirt for free."

Roe ignored them, embarrassment burning him from the inside out, eyes stuck on Mack. "I'm so sorry. They tricked me. I was just trying to save your honor. I wasn't jealous or anything. Why would I be? We aren't together. We're just friends, and that's okay. I'm okay. Are you okay?"

Mack's lips turned up in a slow, hot grin. He pulled Roe back into his side and lowered his head to kiss him.

It was Roe's turn to be confused, but Mack's kiss made him forget why he should be confused. The strong arm wrapped around him didn't help clarify anything. He just felt safe and cared for and *wanted* for the first time in a very long time.

Mack's tongue slipped into his mouth, aggressive in his desire. Roe moaned and sunk into him, unable to hold anything back. Their noses brushed each other, almost sweetly, while their mouths devoured one another.

"Dad, what are you doing?" Lacey asked, her voice shrill. "People are watching."

"This is so embarrassing," Daphne added, groaning. "You guys are too old to suck each other's faces in public. This is traumatizing. Renee, I'm going to need a bear of my own now. Can you win me that blue one?"

"Get a room, Dad," Tris said in between his laughter. "Come here, Benji. You don't need to see all that."

"Kiss, kiss," Benji said, giving Mack and Roe a kiss each before letting Tris take him.

Lacey tried to stifle a laugh but couldn't. "I can't believe you, Dad."

Roe's face felt like it was on fire, and he looked around for any distraction. "How about those food trucks?"

$\mathcal{M}$ack wasn't sure what had caused the change between him and Roe, but he was certain that he didn't mind it one single bit. He followed Roe in a daze, vaguely aware they were headed to the food trucks and were surrounded by Wilsons and Wilson adjacents.

"Lacey," Ernie said, eyes cool.

"Ernie," she frostily replied.

Abel snickered and worked with Justin and Caden to push two of the wooden tables near the food trucks together. "Are you two seriously still doing that whole *I love to hate you* thing?"

They both glared at Abel.

"Okay, okay," Abel said, holding his hands up. "Forget I said anything."

"Lobster rolls?" Roe looked at one of the food trucks, surprised. "They serve lobster at a summer festival?"

"It's a Maine thing," Eduardo said, laughing. "They serve lobster everywhere."

"I'll get us some," Mack said, clearing his throat. "Drinks too."

Abel winced. "That reminds me. Justin and I are supposed to take over at the pub's booth in a few minutes."

Justin groaned. "Come on. Let's go get it over with. We can have lunch after."

By the time Mack came back to the table with a mound of food, everyone was seated, and Daphne and Renee had joined them.

Wally scooted over so Mack could sit next to Roe.

"You're Justin's brother, Griff, and you're Abel's brother, Ernie?" Roe asked, eyeing the two men. "And Nico here is an honorary Wilson and lives with Gramps and his wife?"

"Don't worry if you can't keep it all straight," Eduardo said, shrugging. "By the time you move here, you'll have it all figured out."

"You're moving here?" Mack asked, pleased.

Roe flushed as he met Mack's gaze. "The kids like it here a lot."

Daphne hugged her new bear. "Yeah, Dad. Let's pretend that kiss has nothing to do with why you really want to move here. Playing make believe is fun."

Renee snickered. "Hug your emotional support bear and leave him alone."

Daphne buried her face against the stuffed animal with a groan. "I can still see it."

"We need drinks, don't we?" Mack asked, voice gruff. "I'll go get us some drinks."

He stumbled a bit getting up from the table, but made a quick exit. He had been waiting in line for a few moments before he noticed Lacey standing at his side.

She watched him, eyes bright with laughter. "I've never seen you like this, Dad."

Mack shrugged sheepishly. "That kiss took me by surprise."

"Are you into him?" she asked, nibbling her lip. "You

haven't dated anyone since Dad passed. I just thought you weren't interested in that anymore."

"No one wants to be alone," he said, pulling her into a hug. "I haven't been unhappy alone, but I like Roe a lot. We've talked for hours every evening since he arrived. He's a good listener and a good friend."

"Is that all?" she asked, a little smirk playing across her lips.

Mack groaned, his face heating up. "He's also handsome and kind. I like being around him, and that kiss was—"

"Okay, okay." She held up her hands. "I'm surprised but in a good way. His kids are nice too. I think Renee wants to adopt Daphne, but I'll try to rein her in."

Mack chuckled. "We'd miss her if you stole her."

They moved forward with the line.

"Have you all heard anything about Roe's case?" Lacey asked after a moment.

"Cain called a few days ago." Mack sighed. "They arrested the man who tried to run him off the road, but he posted bail. He wasn't talking, but Wally's company traced him back to Gabriel. They have been meeting up at a bar near James's company for the past three months."

"Are the police taking it seriously this time?"

Mack was quiet for a moment, thinking hard. "Not really, and I don't understand why not. They seem to be playing it off as if Roe arranged everything to garner attention. They even tried to talk Cain into dropping the charges."

"That doesn't make any sense." Lacey scowled. "There has to be something else going on."

"They're looking into it. All we can do is keep Roe and the kids safe and happy."

"Tris leaves for college next week," Lacey said, sounding sad. "I wish I would have come by when they first arrived. I wanted to give them space, but I really like them."

Mack hugged her again. "You're a good one, Lacey baby."

She rolled her eyes. "I'm not a baby anymore."

"You'll always be my baby."

They fetched drinks and brought them to the others. Ernie was in the middle of describing a few of the outfits he'd knitted for one of the festival events coming up.

"Arthur looks so cute in his bumblebee costume," Ernie said. "I actually used one I'd made for Maury and just resized it. I really hope someone wants to adopt him."

"He's a rabbit?" Roe asked, clearly trying to look uninterested but failing miserably.

"He is," Ernie took one of the drinks from Mack. "I think Henry said he was a lionhead mix. He's white with a black stripe down his back. He ended up at the animal sanctuary when his owner died. The poor boy was in pretty bad health, but he's doing well now."

Mack sat beside Roe and pulled a side salad from one of the food trays in the middle of the table. He opened it and put some of the mixed greens in the guinea pig stroller, mentally calculating if there was enough space for a rabbit. He wasn't sure if it was all right to put rabbits and guinea pigs together, so they might end up carrying Arthur. The interest in Roe's eyes told him they would be going home with a rabbit, one way or another.

Wally nudged his side. "Roe needs that rabbit."

"I'll see what I can do," Mack whispered back.

After a long day at the festival, Mack finally found himself alone with Roe once the kids were in bed. They sat in his studio, Roe lounging in his chair and Mack perched on the ottoman.

"How's your leg?" he asked. Roe looked like he was about

to fall asleep. Arthur sat in his lap, already dozing. The costume had come off the rabbit as soon as they got home, but the dang thing was still cute as a button. He wasn't very big, but he looked like a ball of white fluff. He sure liked Roe too.

"It's a little sore, but it was worth it." Roe gave him an uncertain look. "Are we going to talk about the kiss?"

"I think we need to." Mack let Mmrr jump onto his lap and settle down. He stroked the top of her head, enjoying the purrs rumbling through her.

"I really like you," Roe said, sighing. "I don't want to lose your friendship, but I won't lie. I want more."

"I do too," Mack said quietly. "I didn't realize it until you kissed me, but it felt right. I haven't wanted to be with anyone since Darren died, but it feels different with you." *Like the ground thawing with the warmth of spring*, he thought, wincing at his flowery thoughts.

Roe smiled softly. "I haven't even thought of anyone romantically since my divorce. There's been no time. Do you want to try a relationship? With me?"

Mack thought for a moment, peeling back the instant want and considering what lay behind it. He wasn't getting any younger, but he wasn't ready for the grave either. Having the right person beside him was an addicting thought. Roe felt like the right person, but . . .

"I'm at least ten years older than you," he said, forcing the words out. "I'm not the most eligible bachelor in Hobson Hills, despite what you saw today."

Roe snorted. "There is no convincing me that you're not a catch, Ian. I've already spent too much time with you to know that's a lie. You're kind and funny. Handsome and sexy both. My kids already adore you." He bit his lip. "I'll be honest and tell you that putting myself out there again is frightening. I'd given up on the idea of a partner." He reached out and took Mack's hand. "In the end, though, I know you're worth the risk. Do you think you can put up with my drama? What about the kids? Are we too much?"

Mack shook his head, wanting to laugh. "You and the kids are great. It's not exactly a burden to spend time with you all. I can't think of anything better than today, everyone all together and having fun."

Roe looked relieved as he leaned back in his seat. "I'm going to have to tell Cain that I love it here, aren't I? He's going to be so smug."

"He's earned it, hasn't he?" Mack pulled Roe's hand to his lips. "Besides, Caden told me he already sent a video of our kiss to him."

"That's why he's called me so many times." Roe groaned. "I suppose I should call him back."

Mack chuckled. "I'll get you some tea while you do that. Decaf. Tell him about the pet matchmaking event. It's a shame he wasn't here. He'd have ended up with that cat in the business suit."

Roe nodded, face solemn. "They would be the perfect fit. Like me and Arthur. Fergie belongs to everyone, the guinea pigs belong to Fergie, and Mmrr belongs to herself. Arthur's all mine. I'm not sharing, and you can't make me."

Mack laughed as he stood. "Yes, sir."

His cell rang, and he sighed. "This late in the evening, that will be work. Rain check on the tea?"

"Absolutely." Roe yawned. "I'm about to fall asleep anyway."

Mack forced himself to answer the phone instead of leaning forward to kiss a sleepy Roe. "McKenzie."

"Sheriff, we have a situation," Parker said solemnly.

"Does it have anything to do with Bigfoot or knitting shenanigans?"

Roe snickered.

"Not this time," Parker said. "We got a call about a domestic at the Scotts' house. When we got here, we found Mrs. Scott in the kitchen. She's been beaten pretty badly. The EMT's got her now, but they aren't sure she's going to make it to the hospital."

"And Eugene Scott?" Mack asked, hands shaking with fury. They had been watching the couple closely for a long time now. Eugene and Layla just happened to wear a perfect mask for the rest of the town. Those in the know were aware of all the cracks in that mask. Mack just hoped Layla didn't die now that it was broken.

"Eugene's missing. We found the kids hiding up in the treehouse in the backyard. Tommy got them out of there as soon as the fighting started."

"Good." Mack ran his hand over his face, suddenly exhausted. "I'm on my way. Put an APB out for Eugene."

"Yes sir."

Mack ended the call and shared a look with Roe. "Being the sheriff really is about more than parking tickets."

Roe nodded. "I heard what he said. I hope that's okay."

"It'll be around town before the morning." Mack sighed. "I need to get out there."

"How many kids are there, and where will they go?" Roe asked. "I'm a certified foster parent in Georgia if that makes any difference."

It took a moment for Mack to catch up to what Roe was saying. Then, it took him a longer moment to stop grinning. "You would do that?"

"If it's all right," Roe nodded. "I'll move Benji in with Tris and my stuff in with Daphne. That will open one room for them. They'll probably want to be together, won't they? At least at first."

Mack leaned forward and kissed him, unable to resist. The sweet man's mouth opened beneath his, and the kiss deepened. Mack let himself get lost, enjoying the stirring passion, even as the feel of another person's lips on his made him feel secure in a way that he hadn't felt in a long time. He wasn't alone, and Roe was the exact right person for him.

He reluctantly ended the kiss. "There are two of them. Tommy is sixteen, and Beth is twelve."

"I'll take care of it," Roe said, stroking Mack's cheek. "Go do what you need to do."

Mack hurried out the door, leaving Roe to explain the situation to Wally and the kids. During the quick drive, Parker called him to let him know Layla had coded before they reached the hospital. It was officially a homicide.

The Scotts lived on a few acres outside of town. The white house with gray trim normally looked picture-perfect, but at night, with the police lights flashing, it was a macabre sight. The kitchen was a mess; chairs were turned over, dishes were broken, a large puddle of blood stood out against the white patterned tile. Dinner was a congealed mess in the middle of the table. One plate of food sat at the head of the table, and one bite was missing from the meatloaf. Three other places were set, but the plates were clean and empty.

Tommy stood right outside the kitchen entrance, arms wrapped around his younger sister. He was pale, eyes focused on the pool of blood.

Mack nodded to Parker and stood between the kids and the scene. "Hey, Tommy. Let's go in the living room, okay?"

Tommy shook his head, eyes dazed. "We aren't allowed in there. The carpet just got cleaned."

Mack eyed the spotless living room across the hall from the kitchen. The white carpet gleamed in the low light. The room didn't look lived in, just a model room out of a magazine.

"How about the steps?" he asked, guiding the two kids to the bottom of the stairway.

Tommy nodded and sat down with Beth beside him. The younger girl hadn't looked up at all; her face stayed buried against her brother's shoulder.

"Did Parker tell you about your mom?" Mack asked, hating the conversation already.

Tommy nodded again, swallowing hard.

"Child services are on their way," Parker said, his voice soft. "Michelle is a friend of mine. She's good people and will get you settled somewhere safe."

Tommy ignored them and laid his head on top of Beth's. "He killed her."

Mack knelt down, keeping eye contact with the teen. "You want Beth here for this?"

"I saw it too," Beth whispered, peeking down at him. Her cheek was bruised, and one eye was already swollen.

Mack bit back a curse. "Parker, can you grab another EMT? Ms. Beth here needs to be checked out."

Parker nodded, his eyes cold, and he turned around to chase someone down.

"Are you hurt, sweetie?" Mack asked, moving to sit on the bottom step of the stairway. "I see you have a bruise there and a big ol' shiner coming up."

"He hit me," she whispered. "It hurt, and Tommy made him stop."

"We were having dinner," Tommy said with his eyes lowered. "He always eats first, but Beth was hungry. We hadn't had lunch because we were at the festival, and Mom doesn't like us eating junk food. Beth just wanted to eat."

"He said I whined, but I didn't whine," Beth said with a trembling lip. "I just asked."

"He got mad and hit her." Tommy looked up, and his eyes were full of rage. "He never hits Beth. Never."

Mack nodded. "He did this time."

"Yeah." Tommy looked back down. "I hit him back. I punched him right in the face."

"Daddy was so mad," Beth said, swallowing hard. "His face turned purple, and I thought he'd kill Tommy."

"Mom"—Tommy's voice broke—"Mom told us to go outside. She started talking to him, trying to calm him down. We went to the treehouse and pulled up the hanging ladder. That way, he couldn't get us."

Mack looked back into the kitchen. Layla Scott had kept his temper busy so he wouldn't hurt her children.

"We heard him yelling," Beth said, hiccupping through her tears. "He killed her, didn't he?"

Mack shared a look with Tommy.

"I saw him do it," the boy whispered. "I saw him through the window. He hit her and kicked her for a while. Every time he headed for the door, he'd stop and go back to her. Then, he looked real surprised for a minute before running out the door."

Mack let Tommy talk him through everything, and he wished the world were a better place, wished he'd been there to protect them.

By the time Michelle arrived, the kids were nestled in Mack's Jeep with their overnight bags packed.

"You sure, Sheriff?" she asked, arching a brow. "You have company right now, and there are a few other temporary options."

Mack shook his head. "I need them under my roof tonight."

She rolled her eyes but smiled at him. "I knew you would say that. I'll come by tomorrow and check in with them."

"Thanks, Michelle." He waved her away and returned to the kitchen. The county forensics team was still processing evidence, and there had been no sign of Eugene Scott anywhere. There were a few ways the situation could go, and none of them were good.

Parker looked up from his clipboard. "I got this, Sheriff, if you want to take the kids home."

"Are you sure?" Mack asked. "It's a lot of paperwork, and Scott is still missing."

"We have eyes and ears out." Parker shrugged. "Nothing to do until we find him. You might as well get rest for tomorrow. I can sleep when I'm off shift."

The drive home was quiet. Tommy and Beth were in shock.

Roe and Wally met them at the door with smiles. Roe still held Arthur like a baby, gently patting the bunny's back, and Fergie danced at their feet, happy to meet new people.

Beth and Tommy pet the dog and said hello.

"I made some mac and cheese," Wally said. "You two want some?"

Beth nodded. "I'm hungry."

"Come on in, little lady. I make top-notch mac and cheese." Wally led the two kids to the kitchen.

"It's not even from a box," Roe said, shrugging. "Who knew he had more skills?"

Mack wrapped his arms around Roe, soaking in his warmth and calming presence.

"Was it bad?" Roe asked.

"Really bad," Mack answered, burying his face against Roe's neck. "Thank you for being here."

"Nowhere else I'd rather be." Roe stroked circles against Mack's back. "We'll get them fed and settled down for the night. Wally already double-checked the security system, and he'll patrol all night. I think he hopes their dad will show up here."

"I do too," Mack said, tightening his arms around Roe. "Don't tell Gramps I said that. He'll want to hide the body."

# CHAPTER 8

Roe set another plate of waffles in the middle of the table. Four teens ate a lot, though he supposed Beth wasn't technically a teenager yet. He was happy to see the Scott children had an appetite. They'd slept heavily the night before too. He'd checked on them on and off, worried that they would be upset. They were, but not to the detriment of their health, thankfully.

Daphne bumped her shoulder into Beth's. "You want more bacon? Wally doesn't burn it like Dad does."

"Wow, thanks, sweetheart," Roe said with a snort before he gave Wally a pleading look. "Can you please make us more bacon?"

Wally grinned and went back to the stove. "Sure thing, boss."

"If only he listened so well all the time," Roe mumbled, sitting down beside Tommy.

Mack came into the room, still on the phone. He was dressed in uniform and looked decidedly yummy. "I'll be there in five, Tanner."

"You need to eat," Roe reminded him once he'd ended the call.

Mack winced. "I don't think I'll have time. Wait a minute. Is that Arthur in your shirt?"

Roe's floofy boy was tucked into his sweatshirt, and the rabbit's head and front paws poked out the top. "He likes to stay close to me."

"Daddy's bunny," Benji said, pouting. "I want to hold."

"Not at the breakfast table, sweetie." Roe stood and grabbed a napkin. He used two waffles and the last of the bacon to make a breakfast sandwich. "Not the healthiest, but it's food."

Mack gave him a soft look and took the sandwich. "Thank you. I'll see you all tonight."

Roe leaned up and gave him a brief kiss, wishing they had time for more. "See you later."

Mack said goodbye to the kids and left, locking the front door behind himself.

After a very quiet moment, Roe looked up from his plate. Daphne and Tris were staring at him with matching grins.

"What?" he asked, flushing.

"Nothing," Tris said with a chuckle. "We're just enjoying seeing you happy."

"It's gross and cute all at the same time." Daphne shrugged. "Anyway, what do you all want to do today?"

Tommy and Beth didn't have time to answer before the doorbell rang.

"Stay here," Wally ordered, handing Roe the spatula. "And don't burn the bacon."

"Yes sir," Roe muttered, scowling.

A few moments later, the kitchen filled with people, most of them familiar. Gramps and his wife, Grammy, herded the crowd into the room.

A pretty black girl went straight to Tommy and hugged him. "I'm so sorry, Tommy. Are you and Beth all right?"

The look of peace on Tommy's face as he hugged the girl back was all Roe needed to know she was important to him. "Thanks for coming, Tali. We'll be okay."

Another teen, a boy, sat beside Beth. "Hey, nice shiner."

She ducked her head and smiled. "Hi, Drew."

"Sorry to interrupt your breakfast," Gramps said, moving to stand at the stove with Roe. "Tali is close to Tommy and was really worried. We were just going to bring her, but the rest of the kids wanted to come too."

"It's no problem. They need friends right now." He took the bacon out of the pan and set it on a plate. "Do you all want some breakfast?"

"I brought some things," Grammy said, smiling. The little gap between her front teeth reminded Roe of Abel and his brother. "Have a seat, sweetheart. I'll finish up breakfast."

Wally poked his head into the kitchen. "I'm going to set up the patio table in the backyard. There's more space there."

"Thanks," Gramps said with his hands on his hips. "Kids, grab plates and drinks and head outdoors. Tali, I'm not sure you can hug Tommy and walk at the same time. Maybe just hold his hand until you're back in a seat. Benji, will you help me make some more waffles? With all that syrup on your face, I know you must be an expert."

"I am," Benji said, nodding furiously. "Love waffles."

Roe chuckled. "Thank you for taking charge, Gramps."

"It's what I do best, young'un." He eyed the bacon. "You have something against pork?"

Roe rolled his eyes and elbowed Gramps. "Hush, you."

Thirty minutes later, the backyard was full of kids with a few adults sprinkled in. Fergie led the guinea pigs around to all his favorite pee spots, Roe had tied balloons around the piggies so they wouldn't get lost in the yard, and Mmrr was hiding in the house avoiding the noise.

Lacey and Renee had arrived shortly after the Wilsons. Lacey and Tris sat together, heads close as they talked about accounting classes. Daphne and Beth kicked a ball around with a few of the teens. Roe had to wipe his eyes when he noticed Daphne keeping her attention on Beth. His daughter had a soft heart and worried about the younger girl.

Benji crawled onto Roe's lap and pet Arthur with a sticky hand. "Daddy's bunny."

"Yes, he is." Roe winced. He'd have to clean Arthur's hair later.

"I have to ask," Gramps said, sitting down beside them. "Why is your dog named Fergie?"

The corgi walked past them at that moment, his round butt shaking.

"Do you really need to ask?" Roe laughed. "He's fierce and confident. Look at that strut."

Gramps chuckled. "I see it now."

The morning passed slowly. It had been a long time since Roe had felt so comfortable in his own skin. There were no hidden motives in the people around him. They were just there to comfort Tommy and Beth. They didn't want anything more from him than friendship. It was good to have true friends. He had thought he had that in Loriston, but he was wrong.

His phone rang, and he saw it was Cain. *Perfect timing*, he thought with a smile.

"Hey."

"How are you?" Cain asked.

"Really well." Roe hugged Benji closer. "Did you get my message from last night?"

"Yes, I went ahead and looked into Tommy and Beth's family. They have a maternal aunt who lives nearby. Social services will likely speak with her first before placing them in a foster home."

"I just want them to be safe," Roe said, sighing. "I can't imagine all they've been through."

"If their aunt can't take them, I'll bet you a thousand dollars that Bennett and Marco Wilson will have them adopted before the end of the year."

"I'm not stupid." The beautiful diverse family currently mingling with his own told him not to take that bet. Tali's adoptive parents had the most beautiful hearts of anyone Roe had ever met.

"Well," Cain said with a sniff. "Be that way. I guess I'll just have to tell you what I dug up about James and Gabriel then."

"Oh, do tell."

"Apparently, when James divorced you, he lost a lot of clients. He may have kept the Dorsey name, but a good portion of the company's clients had been with your grandfathers from the start. They weren't happy with his treatment of you."

"Oh dear." Roe winced. "I can see that making him angry."

"It didn't help that the company's best employees left as well," Cain continued. "James is relatively young to be running a company of that standing. He doesn't have the experience to inspire trust. With that turnover, the company lost a lot of standing."

"So, they're mad at *me*?" Roe asked, rolling his eyes. "Seriously?"

"Looks like it. The timing of their harassment and the changes in the company match up. Now, we have motive, so we are looking into their connection with the police in Loriston. Everything has happened there, and it is a small county. The local police have been very nonchalant from the start."

"Okay." Roe frowned and cuddled deeper in his chair,

nuzzling the top of Benji's head. "Grandpa Roland was friends with the previous sheriff, but they put a new one in several years ago. I don't know him as well."

"We will figure it out. You just stay safe in Hobson Hills."

Roe nibbled his lip for a moment. "Do you think you could have someone pack up the house and ship our things?"

"Why am I not surprised?" Cain asked, laughing.

"Well, you're moving here too," Roe said, grinning. "What did you expect?"

"How did you . . .? Never mind. I don't want to know. I'll find someone to take care of the house. We still need to keep your location on a need to know basis. The driver who tried to kill you, Ned Bollinger, is out on bail, but we have someone watching him. I'm worried James and Gabriel will up their game if they find out you are out of the state. James needs the infusion of cash that gaining custody of the kids would give him. He'd have access to your money."

"That's his endgame?" Roe swallowed hard, suddenly feeling sick to his stomach.

"I think so." Cain sighed. "I shouldn't have said anything. Don't worry about it, Roe. Take care of yourself and the kids, and let me deal with these assholes."

"Gladly, but hurry up. I want you to come meet my new friends. We're the Hot Mess Club, and I really think you should join."

"Fuck me," Cain groaned. "You're already mixed up with *them?*"

MACK DIDN'T MAKE it home until after dinner, and Roe was a little surprised at how much he missed his presence. And his cooking. Wally was a one-trick pony, and they couldn't eat mac and cheese for every meal. Instead, they were left with Roe's limited skills, so it was chef salad for everyone.

Benji ran to the door as soon as Wally opened it. "Daddy says we bunnies, Macky!"

Mack pulled the little boy into his arms and hugged him. "What's this about bunnies?"

Roe rolled his eyes. "I made them eat salad for dinner. It had meat on it, for goodness' sake. You'd think I haven't been feeding him for three years now."

"Want pancakes." Benji pressed his face against Mack's neck. "Please?"

"Hmm." Mack grinned at Roe. "Maybe your daddy spends too much time with Arthur."

Roe gasped and patted the rabbit riding around in his sweatshirt. "A curse upon you for those filthy words."

Benji sighed dramatically. "I'm hungry."

Mack gave Roe a searching look. "Well, Daddy?"

"Oh, fine." Roe stomped his foot. "Feed the little monster, Ian. The others were perfectly happy, I'll have you know."

"Come on, beastie. Let's make some pancakes." He leaned over and kissed Roe's cheek. "I'll have salad if there's any left over."

"There's plenty."

"It's game night, Mack!" Daphne called from the living room. "Come play with us!"

"Be there in a moment," Mack called out.

"Dad, do we still have *Carcassonne* and all the expansions?" Lacey darted into the living room. "I think they'd really like it."

"She said it was Darren's favorite board game." Roe smiled softly. "If you don't mind us playing."

Mack hugged Lacey, squashing Benji between them. "That's a great idea, baby girl. It should be in a trunk in the storage shed out back."

"I'll dig it out." She left, heading toward the back door.

"When did she get here?" Mack asked.

"Right before dinner." Roe followed him into the kitchen. "I invited her and Renee for game night. Just so you know, they were happy with the salad I made too."

"I'm sure the salad is delicious."

Benji made a face then wiggled out of Mack's arms. "I get chair."

"I think that's why he likes pancakes so much." Roe smiled after his son. "He gets to help you make them."

"That kid already owns my heart," Mack said, watching Benji push a chair toward them. "Surprise babies are the absolute best."

"Agreed." Roe leaned back on the counter, resting his ankle. "How was today?"

"All right, but we still haven't tracked down Eugene Scott. I'm starting to wonder if he ran at all."

"What do you mean?"

"We know he took his car, but there's been no sign of him anywhere in Hobson Hills or the other two nearby towns. If he left the area, someone would have seen him. I think he's hunkered down somewhere."

"What are you going to do?" Roe asked, pulling himself up to sit on the counter. "Tommy and Beth are petrified that he's going to come for them."

"We're going to focus on the national park. There are a few roads up there and a ton of hiking trails. Lots of camping and hunting spots."

Benji finally managed to get the chair to them, so Roe changed the topic to a lighter one. "What do you all think about blueberry pancakes?"

"Yummy," Benji said, rubbing his belly.

"Pancakes?" Tris asked, coming into the room. "Will you make us some too, Mack? Tali and her brother Drew are here, so there's eight of us plus Benji. Oh, Wally, do you want pancakes?"

Wally sat nearby, reading a book. He didn't bother to look up. "Second dinner sounds great."

"Heathens," Roe hissed. "You're all heathens." Now he just had to figure out how to ask for pancakes while remaining outraged with everyone else.

A FEW HOURS LATER, Roe finally had some alone time with Mack. They sat in his studio, curled together on Roe's chair. The kids were in bed, and Lacey and Renee had gone home.

"I'm worried about Tommy." Roe nuzzled Mack's neck, taking in the alpha's heavenly scent. The calm it brought him was a little frightening, especially since James's scent had done nothing for him.

"What about? He and Beth seem to be doing all right, all things considered."

Roe leaned back so he could meet Mack's gaze. "He isn't doing anything wrong. It's just that I find him sometimes when he's alone, and he looks so mad, like he can't keep all the emotion inside and wants to break the world in half. Tali and Beth both help, but he needs something else. I just don't know what. He's been through so much, and I can only imagine what he's feeling."

"I'll ask Michelle for advice," Mack said, hugging him. "They meet with a therapist next week, but she may have an idea of something more. We just need to make sure they know we're there for them, no matter what."

"Yes." Roe nuzzled Mack's neck again. "You smell so good."

"Really? I haven't showered yet." Mack cupped Roe's cheek. "May I kiss you?"

Roe smiled softly. "Anytime, anywhere."

Mack kissed him, his lips soft and warm, tongue slipping inside Roe's mouth.

Roe settled into Mack's embrace, letting his safety and strength surround him. The small fire in his belly grew slowly with every touch of Mack's lips.

Mack moved his mouth to Roe's neck. "I could kiss you all night."

"Promises, promises." Roe tilted his head, making more room for Mack. He moaned when Mack bit his shoulder through his T-shirt, his body hot and full of want and his dick painfully hard. "It's been a while, Ian. If you keep this up, I'm going to embarrass myself."

"Now who's making promises?" Mack spread his legs and adjusted Roe on his lap, careful of his injured ankle. They rocked against each other, breathing heavily in between wet kisses.

Mack's hands slid to Roe's ass, and he pulled him tight against him, rubbing his hard dick against Roe's erection.

The heat built as they moved, drowning in a sea of sensation. It didn't take long for them to find release.

"Oh dear," Roe said, panting. "I came in my pants."

Mack huffed a laugh against Roe's neck. "You're not the only one."

# CHAPTER 9

"He disappeared?" Mack asked again, looking around the kitchen one more time to make sure no one else was there.

Wally nodded. "Ned Bollinger skipped bail. The tail my company had on him lost him in Virginia, so we know he's heading north."

"Why didn't the police pick him up as soon as he left Georgia?"

"Local police didn't report it. My company called it in to the state police. By the time they caught up, Bollinger was gone."

"Of course." Mack ran his hands through his hair. They were driving Tris to school today, and Roe was already a bundle of nerves. He really didn't want to be the one to bring Bollinger up.

"We should be safe on the road, but can you have someone watch your house while we're gone?" Wally asked. "If he's heading north, then there's a chance he knows where Roe has been."

"Parker is petsitting. I'll let him know." Daphne and Benji

were both staying with friends instead of making the five-hour drive, so they would be safe. "Do you think Roe would stay here? From what I understand, it's common knowledge that Tris is going to Harvard. All it would take is James or Gabriel going to the website to see when classes start. They would know Roe would be there with Tris."

"You can ask him," Wally said, doubtful.

Mack sighed and went in search of his omega. He had worried for Roe before they decided to try a relationship. Now, he was sure he'd have an ulcer by the time things were settled.

Roe was sitting with Tris in the studio. He held a small 8×8 framed painting. Mack looked over his shoulder and admired the portrait. It was of Roe and the kids, a traditional oil and canvas painting. Around the family, bits and pieces of memories were worked into the painting. A blue and white bow made from a baby blanket, a movie stub from years ago, a silver button, a birthday candle, pieces of a calendar, and two lovely vintage lockets.

"The silver locket was your grandmother's," Roe said, wrapping his arm around Tris's shoulder. "I put a picture of Dad and her in there. The gold one at the bottom has a picture of Grandpa Roland and Grandpa Ben. I don't want you to forget us while you're figuring yourself out. We'll always be with you."

Tris hugged Roe tightly. "Thank you, Dad."

Mack stepped back and let them have their moment, knowing without a doubt that Roe would be in the car with Tris on the way to Cambridge.

And two hours later, that was exactly where Mack was. Mack drove while Tris and Roe sat in the back talking about class schedules and dorm rooms. Wally sat in the passenger seat texting his boss for updates as they searched for Bollinger. The back of the SUV was full of clothes, books, and all the other odds and ends that came with dorm life. There was also a pet carrier in between the two omegas, as Roe couldn't be parted from his darling Arthur. Mack hoped with everything in him that Bollinger wasn't searching for Roe, but he knew it was the likeliest scenario.

They stopped for lunch in Portsmouth then made the rest of the drive quickly to avoid the evening traffic. The campus was nice, but Mack felt distinctly out of place. The buildings were old, and the arriving students were fresh-faced babies. It could have been Harvard's reputation getting to him, but the place felt *elite* in a wealthy kind of way.

Tris was lucky enough to get a single room in a suite, though the communal bathroom was down the hall. He would share the suite with four other people, two of whom he knew. Mack wished *he* knew the other kids. He was starting to feel Roe's nerves. It was going to be hard to leave Tris.

They helped him set up his minifridge and unpack before taking him to dinner. Cambridge was a nice city, but it was so much bigger than Mack was used to. It had been a while since he'd left Hobson Hills, and he had forgotten how insulated his home was.

"I'll come home for all the breaks, Dad," Tris said, grinning. "I promise. Eat your steak and be happy."

Roe sighed. "It *is* a good steak."

Mack grunted and took another bite. The steakhouse they were at had required a reservation and didn't include prices on the menu. He didn't think he had ever been somewhere this fancy before. The pub back home was better and cheaper. Maybe it wasn't a fair comparison to the fancy place though. They didn't have Ernie's husband cooking for them.

After dinner, Roe grabbed the bill before Mack could, and they left the restaurant. It was nice outside, the heat of the day cooling as the sun set. The street was still busy, and it took them a moment to find the SUV.

Mack wasn't sure what had made him move. Had it been the angry-looking man standing behind the car next to them? The glare of the streetlight on a muzzle?

Or had it been the crack of a bullet firing?

Instinct drove Mack to shove Roe behind him. The next instant, something punched into his shoulder, spinning him around to face Roe.

Roe cried out and caught Mack before he tumbled to the ground.

"I'm calling 911," Tris said, trembling. He scooted up to Mack's other side and helped support him.

Mack looked around, shock driving the pain away for the moment. "Wally?"

"He's chasing that man," Tris said in between giving their location to the operator.

"Shh," Roe whispered, holding him tightly. "Here, sit down."

Mack slid onto the back seat of their vehicle and startled when Roe pressed something to his shoulder.

"Are you all right?" he asked, looking over his omega, making sure he hadn't been hit.

"'Are you all right,' he asks," Roe muttered, voice shaky.

"I think I got shot," Mack said, his shoulder beginning to burn as pain settled into him.

"Yeah, you did." Roe kissed his forehead and pressed harder against his shoulder. "If you die, I'll hate you forever, Ian McKenzie. Do you understand? What's your middle name? I need it to properly yell at you, damn it."

"Don't want you to hate me," Mack mumbled, vision dimming.

～

HE WOKE to muffled voices and the sound of Roe crying. Mack knew that was *wrong*. Roe should never cry. The familiar smell of *hospital* sent a shiver through him.

"Roe?" he said, voice barely a croak.

"Ian," Roe took his hand, squeezing it. "You're awake."

"What happened?"

"Ned-fucking-Bollinger shot you."

"Dad." Tris sounded scandalized.

"You're all right?" Mack asked, remembering the sound of the gun and Roe's scream. His eyes focused on Roe's face. His omega looked unreasonably pissed.

"Am I all right?" Roe asked, voice barely above a whisper. "The man I adore got shot because of me!"

Mack couldn't stop his smile. "You adore me?"

"*I'm* going to shoot you." Roe threw his hands up and paced next to the hospital bed.

Wally cleared his throat. "Roe, will you come with me to get some water for Mack? He's probably thirsty."

Roe glared at the bodyguard with a scowl. "Of course he's thirsty. He had to have surgery because he got shot. By Ned-fucking-Bollinger."

Wally gave Mack a sympathetic look and guided Roe from the room.

Mack almost closed his eyes to sleep some more, but Tris's sniffles drew his attention.

"Tris? What's wrong, son?"

Tris sat on the edge of the bed and took his hand. "You saved Dad's life."

"He's all right." Mack bit back a yawn. "Wally and I will keep him safe. You just worry about getting good grades."

"I'm not going to school." Tris shook his head. "I'm not leaving Dad."

"Think again." Mack gave him as stern a look as he could

muster. "Your dad will be talking about shooting *you* if you tell him that. I promise I'll keep him safe, Tris."

"What about you?" Tris wiped his eyes. "I've never seen Dad as happy as he is with you. He loves us, and I know we make him happy, but you make him come alive. If you die, I'm scared that he'll never smile again."

Mack wasn't sure what to say to that. Life was never a certainty. Darren had taught him that.

"I'll let you in on a little secret, Tris. You can't live if you're worried about death, whether it's your own or someone you love. It's inevitable. Life is the tricky part that you have to work to get right. If you let fear control you now, it'll make figuring that life out a hell of a lot harder."

"What if I go to school and Dad dies?" Tris asked, tears falling again. "What if you die? What if I never see you or Dad again?"

"Don't you let what-ifs haunt you," Mack said. "I promise that we'll do everything in our power to stay safe and happy. You need to promise us the same. That's what we can do. That's what we can control."

Tris nodded and closed his eyes. "I hate *that man* so much. Why does he get to do this to us?"

The door opened, and Wally and Roe came back inside. Roe filled a glass for him and helped him sip some water.

"The doctor said you'd be all right." Roe set the glass on the table next to the bed. "They pulled the bullet out, and it didn't hit anything too important. You'll be out of the hospital by tomorrow. You better thank the heavens it wasn't worse. I'll kill you if you die."

Tris chuckled. "Dad, leave him alone."

"Never."

"What happened with Bollinger?" Mack asked after another drink.

"Wally got him," Roe said, smiling fondly at the bodyguard. "Practically sat on him until the police arrived."

"He's in jail with no bond," Wally said, leaning against the wall. "This isn't small-town Loriston, Georgia. He has no friends in high places here. No one to convince the police it was just a big ol' joke. I give it maybe two days before reality sets in and he turns on James and Gabriel."

"Good," Mack said, yawning again. He let his eyes close and drifted off to sleep, satisfied that Roe was angry, not sad. Curses were much better than tears.

IT WAS dark out the next time he woke up. Tris was gone, and Wally snored from the chair in the corner. Roe sat in the chair next to the bed, his dark eyes watching him.

"Hey, sweetheart," Mack said, reaching for the water glass.

Roe scooted forward and helped him take another drink.

"Did Tris go back to campus? Are you feeling better?" Mack asked.

"Tris told me about your talk with him." Roe leaned forward and pressed his forehead to Mack's, rubbing their noses together. "Thank you. He's been through a lot, and he needed that push."

"I just hope I said the right thing."

Mack felt Roe's smile against his cheek. "You always seem to know what to say."

He snorted. "Lacey would tell you differently."

"I don't know what to say now," Roe whispered.

"What's wrong, sweetheart?"

"You were sleeping, and Tris went back to campus," Roe began, leaning back so he could look at him. "I watched you as you lay there hurting. Because of me."

"Roe—"

"I talked to the nurses and paid the hospital bill," Roe interrupted him. "I told Wally we were leaving. That we'd pack up our things and move out of your house. Lacey could come and bring you home."

"No." Mack struggled to sit up. "Don't do that."

Roe gently pressed him back down. "I didn't get past the door, Ian. I'm too selfish to leave you, even if you would be better off."

"I would never be better without you," Mack said, bringing Roe's hand to his lips. "I hate the thought of you and the kids leaving, even if it's just to move to your own place in Hobson Hills. The house wouldn't be home anymore. I need you for that to happen."

Roe's dark eyes were luminous in the dimly lit room. "I don't want to leave you. I think I'm in love with you."

Mack gave a weak laugh. "Hell, it's too soon, isn't it? That's what everyone would say, but I knew when I met Darren in high school that first day. Sometimes, it happens fast, right? I think I knew I loved you when you kissed me at the festival."

Roe laughed roughly and leaned down to kiss him. "I love you, Ian William McKenzie."

Mack cocked his head. "My middle name isn't William."

"That's the name I gave you when I was yelling at you in the ambulance."

Mack chuckled. "I love you too, Roland Quincey Dorsey."

"That is very much not my middle name."

"Close enough," Mack said as he pulled him down into a kiss.

*a* few days later, they were back in Hobson Hills. Roe sipped his tea and surveyed his new kingdom. The studio was lit with sunshine and packed full of supplies and bits of interesting items he'd collected over the years to use in future projects.

Two completed pieces were displayed above his chair. He and Harper had finished their shadow box, and it was gorgeous. Harper had added his own flair by carving and shaping the box to make it appear as if it were a tree trunk. The hole in the painting was so lifelike, Roe thought a squirrel might be tempted to make it a home. Harper had even carved the acorns and wooden leaves to add into the painting.

The gallery in Savannah wanted it, so it would be boxed up and shipped soon. The going price was $25,000, and they already had an interested buyer. The profits would be split between him and Harper. They had another piece in the planning stage that would be just as enchanting.

The other completed piece hanging on his wall was his favorite creation of all time. It was oil and acrylic with lace and leather pressings. Mack's bare back and broad shoulders dominated the painting, flowing into an enticing hint of his beautiful firm ass. He looked back over his shoulder, his eyes smoldering with heat.

"I can't look away," Renee said, horrified.

"He painted a nude of my dad," Lacey wailed. "Oh my god, his eyes are following me."

Roe patted her shoulder and sat in his chair, propping his boot up on his ottoman. Two more weeks and it could come off.

He grabbed his sketch book and flipped it to the right page. "Okay, here's what I'm thinking for you and Renee. Basically, an oil painting collage using a press of your invitation, pressings of your flowers, and bits of other mementos. I want your faces close enough your noses touch, a single veil flowing over your faces. Harper can carve a driftwood frame. What do you think?"

Renee's eyes widened as she studied the sketch. "I love it. I'd be happy just with the sketch. Damn, you have a lot of talent."

"Roe, it's beautiful." Lacey sat beside him and pulled him into a hug. "Thank you." She kissed his cheek. "Not just for the picture either. Dad loves you."

"I'm sorry he got sho—"

Lacey covered his mouth. "Stop apologizing. The important part is you're both okay."

"I just want you to know," Renee said, handing him back his sketchbook, "We're not making our wedding a double wedding. You'll have to get your own."

Roe flushed. "Oh, ha, ha. Are you all sure you're okay with watching, Ian, Benji, and Arthur? Daphne is at Birdie's house, so it will just be Ian and the babies, and Ian should sleep through the afternoon."

"He does know that Arthur is just a rabbit, right?" Renee asked Lacey, side-eyeing him.

"He's my floofy baby." Roe set his teacup down and stood again. "This horse farm thing better be worth it. All I want to do is crawl in bed with Ian and stay there."

"Ew, ew, ew." Lacey ran from the room, her nose wrinkled in distaste.

"Just for cuddles!" he called after her. "Geez, he was shot a few days ago. We'll have to wait at least a week before we get too active!"

Renee bent over, laughing hard.

He left her to it and kissed Benji and Arthur goodbye. Fergie and the guinea pigs were napping, and Mmrr was still pouting about Tris leaving. She had taken to following Mack around, so she might make him her human. With cats, though, one never really knew what would happen.

Tommy and Beth came down the stairs right before he started up them. "Are you two ready to go? Wally's going to let me drive."

"No, I'm not." Wally pocketed the keys and opened the door.

Beth giggled and followed behind the large man. Her bruises were healing, and her spirit was bouncing back faster than Roe had thought it would.

Tommy, however, was having a harder time. The fact that Eugene Scott was still missing didn't help matters. The boy tried to appear *normal*, but he was struggling.

Roe squeezed Tommy's shoulder. "Let's go pet some horses."

"You sound a little skeptical there, Ro-Ro," Tommy said, giving him a half grin.

"Not at all." Roe sniffed. "I just prefer petting rabbits."

"Is Arthur your favorite child?"

Roe fluttered his lashes. "I love all my children equally. Is

Arthur the easiest to deal with? Yes. Yes, he is."

Tommy shook his head and went out the door.

The drive out of Hobson Hills was almost too picture perfect. They passed a cute country store called Farm Fresh and several fields of corn and hay. He thought he recognized Gramps on a tractor, but he couldn't be sure.

The horse ranch was just as picturesque as everything else. There were two large barns surrounded by fenced fields. A short distance away, an old mill with a water wheel sat prettily in the middle of a large creek.

He spied a few people coming and going from the barn, one of which was Min's father, Dean. Most were clearly employees, but he noticed several who seemed out of place. One was a young, timid woman riding a palomino, and there were two men who looked stiff and unsure as they brushed another horse down.

Then, his attention was caught by a brown horse out in the field. He was rolling around in a dust patch with his legs in the air.

Roe pressed his face to the window and laughed. "Look at that weirdo."

Tommy looked a little more excited at the sight. "Huh, does he know he's a horse and not a dog?"

They parked and met the therapist, Diane, in front of the largest barn. A young man stood beside her, smiling a familiar, gap-toothed smile.

"I spy a Wilson," Roe sing-songed.

Diane snorted. "Yes. This is Noah Wilson. He owns the ranch and will help introduce Beth and Tommy to the horses. He's deaf, but he's an excellent lip-reader. Please face him when you speak. I can sign to translate as well."

"Hello, Noah," Roe signed. He'd learned ASL when he was in college. He wasn't fluent, but he could get by if he needed to—and it was nice to stretch his fingers.

Noah's smile widened. "Hi. Are you Sheriff McKenzie's hot younger man? Abel's told everyone about you."

Roe groaned. "Seriously?"

Diane rolled her eyes. "Come on, kids. Let's talk a little bit, then Noah can introduce you to the PB&J club."

"Another club?" Roe asked and signed. "How many can one town have?"

Noah snorted a laugh. "They're my miniature horses. Peanut, Butter, and Jelly."

"Nice," Beth said, eyes widening with excitement.

Diane led the kids away, and Roe stuck his hands into the pockets of his shorts, feeling a little out of place. Wally leaned back against the car, his gaze roaming.

Noah nodded toward the field with the rolling horse. "Do you want to meet Stinkbug?"

"Yes, please," Roe signed and followed him. The ranch had a peaceful air about it. Flower beds lined the barns, and large chestnut trees shaded the walk ways.

"How many people come here for therapy?" Roe signed.

"We get new patients often, but most only stay a few months before they're able to move on to other modes of therapy. That said, we have sixteen regulars who have been coming each week for the past two years."

"Wow." Roe leaned against the fence and watched Stinkbug run to them. "I thought it was a temporary type of therapy."

Noah held his hand out, and the horse nuzzled his palm, searching for a treat. "It's a lot more helpful than most people think. Horses have a way of connecting with people so they don't feel so alone in whatever they're dealing with. I think spending time with my uncle's horses saved my mental health"—he gestured to his head—"after I lost my hearing. I had a lot of family trouble to work through too."

Roe leaned closer and stroked Stinkbug's neck.

"Here, why don't you give him a brush?" Noah asked, hopping over the fence. "There's a set of brushes over by the water trough."

The next hour passed quickly as Roe learned about the different kinds of brushes and what worked best to get dirt out of a naughty horse's coat. Stinkbug was a character. At one point while Roe was combing his mane, the horse had stolen the wallet from his back pocket.

It was nice to let go for a while. Stinkbug listened raptly as Roe told him all about Mack and Lacey. How Mack got shot and how Lacey was getting married. How Roe was in love with a man after only knowing him for about a month. How everything was so much better with Mack than it had been with James.

Talking through his thoughts cleared up a few things for him, and before Roe knew it, Diane and the kids were back and ready to go. Tommy's eyes were a little swollen from crying, but he looked loads lighter then when they arrived.

That decided things for Roe. "I'll meet you all at the car, okay? I need to talk to Noah for a minute."

He walked off before anyone could change his mind, though he felt Wally following a distance behind him. Not like he could move very fast.

Noah was shoveling out a stall in the smaller barn. He looked up when Roe came into his line of sight.

"Hey, Roe. Did you need anything?" Noah asked.

Roe shuffled from foot to foot. "My grandpas would have really liked your ranch," he signed.

A proud smile spread across Noah's face. "Thank you. I think we do a lot of good. For people *and* horses."

"I donated to the animal sanctuary in Hobson Hills last week," Roe went on, letting out a slow breath. "I would really like to donate to the ranch, if you wouldn't mind."

Noah gave him a surprised look. "Yeah, that would be

great. We run on grants mostly, but more insurance companies are paying for equestrian therapy then they used to. Horses eat a lot, though. Donations are always welcome."

Roe wiggled happily. "Perfect. I'll send a check over tomorrow. We'll be back, Noah. I have more to tell Stinkbug, and I think it helped the kids."

"Thanks." Noah waved as Roe left the barn.

Wally smirked at Roe. "I'd bet you my next paycheck that he won't be expecting your check to be over a hundred dollars."

"I donated $50,000 to the animal sanctuary." Roe shrugged. "I'm thinking at least that much for Noah's ranch. If I'm going to live in Hobson Hills, I'm going to take care of and invest in my community."

"Freaking millionaires," Wally said, shaking his head.

Roe sniffed. "Loriston doesn't realize what it's lost."

A little while later, they were home. Tommy went straight to Fergie and the guinea pigs while Beth went to make a snack.

Roe smiled when he saw Lacey and Renee in his studio fingerpainting with Benji and Arthur. Well, pawpainting in Arthur's case. He left them to it and went upstairs to hunt down his alpha.

Mack was sitting up in his bed reading a book. He looked so cute in his reading glasses, and Roe's fingers itched for his drawing pencils. He'd only been staying in Mack's room for a couple of nights now, but it was nice, with warm sand-colored walls and rich-brown blankets on the king size bed.

Mack had even set up beds for both Fergie and Arthur under the window. Mmrr was a white ball of fluff curled against Mack's side on the bed, having decided to help him rest and get better.

"Cain called while you were gone," Mack said, holding his arm out to Roe.

Roe slid onto the bed and cuddled against Mack's free side. "What did he have to say?"

"James and Gabriel have been charged with murder for hire. Bollinger turned on them, just like Wally said he would."

"Yes!" Roe pumped his fist in the air. He slid back off the bed and paced around, his body jittery with the relief running through him. "I'm free, Ian!"

Mack nodded, looking thoughtful. "Cain's pursuing charges against the local police too. Bollinger told him that James paid off the sheriff in Loriston, as well as several of his deputies."

"That makes sense." Roe stared out the bedroom window. "I think I'm going to sell the house in Loriston."

"Good," Mack said, coughing to clear his throat. "You'll stay here, right?"

Roe spun around. "Of course. I thought we settled that at the hospital."

"I love you," Mack said, slumping down in the bed. "If I thought you'd say yes, I'd marry you tomorrow."

Roe's heartbeat sped up, blood rushing in his ears. He had thought Renee was being silly, joking about Roe and Mack getting married. "Why wouldn't I say yes?"

Mack's eyes widened. "Because you haven't known me long and would think I'm crazy for wanting to tie us together."

Roe sat on the bed and cupped Mack's face in his hands. "If I say it's been long enough to know I love you, then why would it not have been long enough to tie myself to you? I'm doing a Darren, Ian. I'm loving you with my whole heart. How about you? I come with four kids and a lot of pets."

"Four kids?"

"Arthur's my baby."

Mack rolled his eyes. "You need to stop hanging around Caden."

"Anyway," Roe said loudly. "Don't you love me, even with all my baggage?"

Mack's smile grew, slowly lighting up his face. "I love you any way I can get you."

Roe licked Mack's bottom lip. "It's a shame we can't celebrate properly."

"We can." Mack pulled him closer. "We just have to celebrate gently."

"Very gently." Roe kissed Mack again, this one more heated. He moved to kneel between Mack's legs, his eyes focused on his alpha's face. Mack's blue eyes warmed as they watched him, and Roe swore they could see into his soul. *Damn, I love this man.*

He slid his hands up Mack's thighs and cupped one hand over his hard, covered dick. He traced the length, enjoying Mack's panting.

"That feels so good."

Roe leaned forward and kissed him, his arms gently wrapping around him as he slid down beside him. "I can't wait to be yours."

"You're already mine," Mack said, smiling against his lips. "Just like I'm already yours. This is just icing on the cake."

Roe chuckled and helped Mack out of his shirt. Then, he took a moment to stroke the muscles of his chest, memorizing every slope, edge, and the feel of his skin.

He moved and straddled his alpha, arching his hips and rubbing against him.

"I didn't expect this, Roe," Mack said as he gripped Roe's hips. "When you first came here, I just wanted to help. I didn't know I needed you so much."

Roe leaned down and kissed him softly. "I didn't expect this either." They awkwardly scrambled out of the rest of their clothes, and Roe laughed when he fell to the side. "I think we're out of practice."

Mack laughed and stroked his back. "We have a lot of missed time to catch up on."

Roe nibbled on his lip and took his time exploring Mack's delicious body, relishing his shudders and moans. He traced warm wet kisses down Mack's stomach and wrapped his hand around his alpha's hard dick.

Mack groaned and arched his hips. Roe took that as an invitation and leaned down and licked the tip of Mack's dick before he started jacking him.

"I don't know how long I can last." Roe pressed their dicks together, admiring the sight, before reaching behind him to finger his hole. "Lube?"

Mack panted, his eyes going dark with need. "Drawer."

Roe leaned to the side and pulled out the lube. "Condom or not? I'm safe."

"Me too." Mack arched up, his dick pressing against Roe's hole. "I need you."

Roe took a moment to carefully stretch and lube his ass, certain he'd implode at any moment.

Mack slowly pushed inside Roe's ass and started a steady rhythm. Roe couldn't think, couldn't speak, he didn't even notice his own moans. Mack felt so right inside him, a part of him.

It was Mack's turn to groan when Roe started riding him. Roe felt his ass squeezing Mack's dick so damn tightly, and his body was burning from the inside out.

After that, it was just heat and movement. Roe forgot who he was and where he was. All he saw was his alpha's sweet blue eyes focused on him.

He held on as long as he could, but the moment Mack's body tightened and he felt the heat of his cum filling him, Roe's seed splattered on their stomachs.

Slowly, their breathing steadied, and Roe leaned down, kissing Mack softly. "Holy moly."

# CHAPTER 11

"Why am I here again?" Roe asked, pulling the strap of the backpack up his shoulder for what felt like the eight hundredth time. "I said I wanted to get back to jogging now that my ankle is healed. This is not that."

"Do you really want those stupid Bigfoot statues to stay in front of Farm Fresh?" Abel asked with a scowl.

"I don't really care," Roe said honestly. "They can sell whatever they want to."

"They won't sell our Dolly Parton T-shirts." Abel snarled. "Aunt Anna said they weren't craft items like the stupid Bigfoot statues. I will *not* let Ernie win."

"Why do we care about Dolly Parton T-shirts?" Wally asked, pulling Roe's pack from his back and adding it to his own.

"I had that." Roe frowned and absently scratched his stomach. Arthur wiggled in the pet carrier strapped to his chest, and he took a moment to kiss the top of his bunny's head.

Wally grunted and ignored him. The bodyguard wasn't

officially *his* bodyguard anymore. Instead, he was settling in Hobson Hills as a new deputy. His connections with his previous employer were a boon for a small county sheriff's office.

"Of course we care about Dolly Parton T-shirts." Abel sniffed. "She's a goddess!"

"You're using the Hot Mess Club for Dolly's Diamonds and Dragons business," Grey said, panting as he caught up to them. "This is some shady shit. Why the hell did we have to hike through the woods instead of just parking here?"

"They'll trace our tire tracks back to us," Abel answered. "And I needed you all because—and don't tell them I said this —most of the members of Dolly's Diamonds and Dragons are either too old or too young to be out here taking care of business. Eduardo, you agree with me, right?"

"Dolly *is* a goddess," the older man said, chuckling. "I don't want to get arrested, though. Better to hike a little than get picked up by the police."

Grey gave Wally a look. "Honestly, I'm more worried about Wally. Isn't he *technically* the police? Do we have to worry about a mole pointing this back to us?"

Abel narrowed his eyes at Wally.

Wally held his hands up. "Hey, it's not like we're *stealing* the statues. This is just a little *redecoration* in the name of our goddess. Besides, we wouldn't have looked for tire prints, not for this."

"We *should* steal them if it will irritate Ernie," Lacey said with a smirk.

"That's the only reason you're here, isn't it?" Abel asked, stomping his foot. "You should be honored."

"We're *not* stealing the statues." Wally sighed. "Wrangling you all is a full-time job."

Roe pulled a purple tutu out of one of the backpacks on Wally's back. "We just dress them in costumes, right?"

"You make it sound so bland," Justin said, snickering. "We're *defiling* the statues, right, Abel?"

"Ernie will be so mad." Abel cackled.

"We could have stayed home and watched *The Mentalist*, Eduardo," Fawn said, wrinkling her nose. "This is ridiculous."

"When a friend asks for help, you help them," Eduardo said, pulling out some more tacky clothes. "Get to defiling, Fawn."

Roe shook his head and pulled out more clothes. He started with the largest Bigfoot. "Caden, come help me."

Caden groaned, but he did as Roe asked. "What if Yeo needs me while I'm out here dressing Bigfoots?"

"Then he'll text you," Roe said. "Now, move it."

It took them about an hour to dress all the statues, mostly because Fawn had brought wine. A lot of wine.

"Aww, they look so pretty." Roe stumbled into Wally, wrapping an arm around his waist. "I like defiling statues."

Wally sighed. "Now what? We hike back? In the dark?"

"Yes," Abel said, a satisfied look on his face. "We have accomplished much here, my friends."

"I can't wait to see Ernie's face." Lacey giggled menacingly.

Caden and Wally led the way back through the dense woods behind Farm Fresh. The cool night air was refreshing, even though Roe's belly itched like crazy.

"Do you think there's poison ivy out here?" he asked, frowning.

"Probably," Grey said with a shrug. "Oh, what if we find Bigfoot while we're here? That would really make Ernie mad."

Roe looked around, chuckling. The light from his flashlight bounced off something white in the trees to his right. "Whoa, what's that?"

His friends stopped and gathered around him, all shining their lights toward the item he'd noticed.

"Is that a shoe?" Caden asked.

"Why would a shoe be out here?" Abel frowned. "No one comes out here. That's why I picked it for our mission."

"Fuck a duck," Grey said, gasping. "That shoe has a foot in it."

Ice crept along Roe's spine as he moved his light a little higher. There *was* a foot in the shoe, and that foot led to a leg.

Wally moved in front of them, blocking their line of sight. "That's enough. I'll call Mack. Abel, get everyone back to the cars and stay there. Wait for the police, then lead them here. Everyone will need to give a statement."

"Is it a body?" Justin asked, sounding shaken.

"Yeah." Wally gave them a grim look. "Get moving."

ROE SAT in the back seat of his car and scratched his stomach again. "I think I got poison ivy."

"Who do you think it is?" Grey bit his bottom lip. "Could it be a hunter?"

"Not in these woods," Abel said, groaning. "Do you think Sheriff McKenzie will ask us why we're out here?"

"He'd be dumb not to, and he's not dumb," Caden said.

"Renee is going to be mad that she didn't get to come," Lacey said, sending another text on her phone.

Several police cars were parked around them, their lights flashing. Roe really didn't think all these people were needed for one little body, but what the hell did he know?

If felt like hours before Mack came to the car.

"Roe, would you like to tell me why you and your friends are stomping through the woods late at night? I thought you were going to the pub. And why is Lacey with you?"

"Lacey is my friend too," Roe said, wincing. He scratched his stomach harder. "We started at the pub, but then Abel asked us to help him with something."

Mack rubbed his hands over his face. "I don't want to know why the Bigfoot statues at Farm Fresh are now dressed like hooker fairies, do I?"

"No, you probably don't," Roe agreed.

"We talked about being Wilson adjacent, damn it."

Roe giggled. "Yeah, I can't help that. You'll have to love me anyway."

"Why are you scratching your belly?" Mack knelt in front of him and took his hands. "Is there something you want to tell me?"

"I think I have poison ivy," Roe said, tilting his head. "Do you know who the body is?"

Mack sighed. "Eugene Scott."

"Oh no," Lacey said, sighing.

"Seriously?" Abel leaned over the front seat. "How could he still be in town for so long and no one saw him?"

"I'm thinking he's been right there since the day he killed Layla," Mack said, shrugging. "Someone killed him."

"This is going to hurt Tommy and Beth," Roe said, biting his lip. "They're just settling in with Lacey and Renee."

"I think they'll be relieved and upset both," Lacey said, giving them a sad look.

"We'll get them through it." Abel patted Lacey's shoulder. "That's what friends do. Now, why don't you tell Sheriff McKenzie more about your itchy belly, Roe?"

Roe rolled his eyes. "Poison. Ivy."

Mack nodded, eyes dancing with laughter. "When's the last time your omega line itched so much?"

"When I was preg . . . Oh my god, Ian. I may be pregnant." Roe's heart sped up as he pulled his shirt up and stared down at his flat belly. His omega line was pink and a little swollen. "I'm forty-seven. This shouldn't have happened."

"Surprise," Grey said, laughing. "Well, Roe, when an alpha and an omega meet and like each other, sometimes they rub—"

Caden covered Grey's mouth. "Shh, now. Shh."

Lacey closed her eyes. "Just when I thought you two couldn't be any more embarrassing. It better be a girl. That's all I'm going to say."

"Ian, what if I'm pregnant?" Roe swallowed hard. "I take naps every afternoon now. I barely have the energy to chase Benji around. That's what Daphne's for. Do you think Arthur will like having a little sister or brother? Oh, I hope it's a girl. No, no, I'll love them no matter what."

Mack leaned forward and kissed him, successfully stopping his rambling. "You all go home. I'll get your statements tomorrow. Roe, make a doctor appointment. I want to know how long I have to work on my cardio so I can chase more babies around."

Roe pressed his cool hands to his warm cheeks. "Yeah, okay. Oh my god. Dead body, maybe having a baby, big day here. Big day."

Roe wanted to wait up for Mack to get home, but he fell asleep as soon as his head hit the pillow. Mack's bed was partly to blame. It was ridiculously comfortable. Their room was a little more cluttered now with Roe's things mixed in with Mack's. Plus, Mmrr had told them she needed a cat tower for their room.

He woke when the bed dipped as Mack crawled in, slipping behind Roe to spoon him. Light filtered through the curtains, falling across a sleeping corgi and rabbit.

"You're just now getting home?"

"Processed the scene and had to wait for forensics to pick up the body." Mack nuzzled the back of Roe's neck. "Called Lacey. She'll keep the kids home today and tell them. Give them time to process before sending them back to school."

"We can take them to visit Diane at the ranch too." Roe's eyes fluttered close as he smiled. "I took a pregnancy test on the way home."

"And?"

"I'm finally getting those six kids, counting Lacey. You and Darren were so considerate to create her for me."

Mack laughed and hugged him tighter. "You're welcome, love."

# CHAPTER 12

*L*acey finished knotting Mack's tie. "You look handsome, Dad. I'm so happy for you and Roe." She smirked. "I'm really glad I didn't talk you into downsizing to an apartment."

Mack snorted. "I told you I needed all those rooms."

With a teen, a toddler, and an infant to house, they put the large home Mack and Darren had bought to good use. Tris even had a room to stay in when he visited from school.

"I can't believe I have a five-month-old sister." Lacey sighed. "Ernie Wilson keeps sending me links to stories of women who were betrayed, robbed, or murdered by their younger sister. I hate him so much."

Mack kissed her forehead. "He's just jealous that he doesn't have a Sherri baby of his own."

Roe had given birth to a healthy little girl. The pregnancy and birth hadn't been easy, but they had something special to show for it. They had wanted to wait for Sherri to arrive before they got married. Mack had barely survived Lacey's wedding, so he had been happy with a long engagement.

"My Sherri baby *is* the best baby in the world, so you're probably right." Lacey spun around, admiring her red dress. Roe had chosen it for her. He'd picked out the clothes for the whole wedding party, all bold colors and unique designs. It was something he hadn't felt comfortable doing in his wedding with James. Mack was happy to let him do as he pleased.

His own tux was royal blue with black lapels and accents. Roe had enjoyed picking it out for him. "How long do we have?"

"About fifteen minutes."

The door burst open, and Benji and Min ran inside. Each boy wore deep-purple newsboy-style suits, complete with hats. They had been inseparable over the last year. Fergie waddled behind them with a teal bow tie hooked to his collar.

"Daddy, it's time, it's time!" Benji crashed into Mack's legs, hugging him tightly. "I gots the rings."

Mack picked him up and hugged him. "Thank you, sweet boy. You look so nice."

"Min looks good too, right?"

"He sure does."

Min preened then knelt to pet Fergie. "Good doggy."

"Is everyone else ready too?" Mack asked, tickling Benji's tummy.

"Yep."

They played for a few more minutes until Renee came to the door to fetch them. She wore an emerald-green gown with black heels. "It's time, Benji. Do you and Min have the rings?"

Benji bounced up and down. "Yes!"

"Come on, Fergie." Min ran out the door, the dog running with him.

Benji giggled and rushed after them.

"Walk! Don't run down the aisle!" Renee yelled. "Dang it. Oh well, that's Barry's problem now."

Abel and Ernie's father had agreed to help plan Mack and Roe's wedding after Lacey and Renee's was finished. He had earned every penny they paid him. It seemed like all of Hobson Hills wanted to see their sheriff married, so it was a very large wedding to plan.

"They'll be fine. Ladies, are you ready to walk me down the aisle?"

Lacey hugged him from one side while Renee snuggled in from the other.

"What a year, huh?" Renee asked. "You met Roe and fell in love, got shot, fostered your future grandbabies, got engaged, had a baby, and gained three more kids. Shew."

"I'm a lucky man." Mack guided them out of the dressing room and into the entry hall of the wedding hall. Roe had chosen an old gristmill for the venue. The place was "rustic chic," or something like that.

Barry waved him over. "Okay, the ring-bearing terrors have made it down the aisle. It's time for our handsome-as-sin sheriff to make his entrance."

Mack rolled his eyes. "Damn annoying Wilsons."

Barry grinned that gap-toothed Wilson grin and kissed his cheek. "You love us."

The familiar notes of "Falling Slowly" began. Mack kissed Lacey's cheek, then Renee's. "Time to marry the man I love."

Lacey sniffled, smiling widely. "I love you, Dad."

"Love you too, baby girl. I'm so proud to have you at my side today."

He led them down the aisle, showing off each young lady on his arm. It looked like most of Hobson Hills had piled into the mill, dressed to the nines, to celebrate with them. Roe and Barry had decorated in bold colors, hanging teal, royal-blue, purple, red, and gold sheer drapes from the ceiling, making the room look like a colorful palace. Fairy lights lit the place up, and deep-green ivy plants lined the rows of seating. Large ferns and colorful orchids accented the front of the hall. Harper and Roe had worked together to create a beautiful wedding arbor carved with roses twined together.

Gramps was there and ready to officiate. Daphne stood with Benji and Min on one side of him. She wore a gold gown with her dark hair pulled up in a bun on top of her head. His grandbabies, Tommy and Beth, stood on Gramps's other side. Each was dressed in their own finery—Tommy in green and Beth in blue. Tommy held his tiny aunt, Sherri, in his arms. Mack and Roe's youngest wore a cute red princess dress. She gurgled happily as he approached.

Daphne wiped her eyes and leaned in for a hug. "Love you, Dad."

"Love you too, Lady Bug." Mack had trouble believing he'd gotten so lucky. His kids were perfect sweethearts.

Lacey sniffled again. "Stop being sweet."

He chuckled and got in position. Renee and Lacey moved to stand with Tommy and Beth. Just in time too. Tris escorted Roe toward him, with Arthur taking the place of a bouquet and wearing a teal tie. Of course Arthur would be there. Mack shook his head with a chuckle then focused on Roe.

Everything disappeared except his beautiful omega.

Roe had chosen a black-and-teal tuxedo with a silk jacket embroidered with roses. He had been worried it was too flashy, but he looked absolutely perfect to Mack.

In seconds, Roe was there beside him, and Mack was lost in his eyes. Lost in his perfect face. Instinct and practice allowed him to reply appropriately when Gramps prompted him, but the only thing he would remember from the ceremony was the warmth of Roe's sweet smile and the feel of his artist hands joined with Mack's.

Before he knew it, Gramps was nudging him. "You're free to kiss your husband, Sheriff."

Roe pulled him down and pressed their lips together. Mack lost himself in the love of his omega, certain that their future would be beautiful because Roe would be at his side.

# AUTHOR'S NOTE

Thank you for visiting Hobson Hills! If you're interested in Gabriel and James's fate and who killed Eugene Scott, keep an eye out for Cain's book, *Admiring His Omega*, coming 2024.

# BOOKS BY C.W. GRAY

*Writing as C.W. Gray*

- **Charybdis Station Chronicles** – *science fiction/fantasy, mpreg*

The Blue Solace Series – series complete
Charybdis Station

- The Hobson Hills Omegas – *non-shifter, mpreg, omegaverse*
- Holiday Omegas – holiday stories from the world of The Silver Isles – *paranormal, mpreg, omegaverse*
- The Silver Isles – *paranormal, mermen, mpreg, omegaverse*

*Writing as Chloe Gray*

- A Little Bit of Perfect – *contemporary, non-mpreg, Daddy/Little age play*

If you would like to keep up with releases join C.W. Gray's Reading Nook on Facebook or visit my website at (https://www.cwgray-author.com).